PENGUIN

MY LOVELY SKULL & ~~OTHER SKELETONS~~

Tunku Halim was born in Malaysia in 1964. He is dubbed Asia's Stephen King. By delving into Malay myth, legends and folklore, his writing is regarded as 'World Gothic'.

His novel, *Dark Demon Rising*, was nominated for the 1999 International IMPAC Dublin Literary Award whilst his second novel, *Vermillion Eye*, is used as a study text in The National University of Singapore's Language and Literature course. His short story has also won first prize in a 1998 Fellowship of Australian Writers competition. In Malaysia, he has had three consecutive wins in the Star-Popular Readers' Choice Awards between 2015 and 2017.

His children's fiction include the Midnight Children trilogy (2021) comprising *A Vanishing, Cemetery House* and *The Midnight World*, whilst his children's non-fiction include *A Children's History of Malaysia* (2019) and *History of Malaysia: A Children's Encyclopedia* (2013).

His other books comprise the short-story collections *The Rape of Martha Teoh & Other Chilling Stories* (1997), *BloodHaze: 15 Chilling Tales* (1999) and *The Woman Who Grew Horns and Other Works* (2001); and the novels *Juriah's Song* (2008), *Last Breath* (2014) and *A Malaysian Restaurant in London* (2015). His non-fiction books, amongst others, include a biography of his late father *A Prince Called "Charlie"* (2018).

My Lovely Skull & Other Skeletons

Tunku Halim

PENGUIN BOOKS

An imprint of Penguin Random House

PENGUIN BOOKS

USA | Canada | UK | Ireland | Australia
New Zealand | India | South Africa | China | Southeast Asia

Penguin Books is part of the Penguin Random House group of companies
whose addresses can be found at global.penguinrandomhouse.com

Published by Penguin Random House SEA Pvt. Ltd
9, Changi South Street 3, Level 08-01,
Singapore 486361

First published in Penguin Books by Penguin Random House SEA 2022
Copyright © Tunku Halim 2022

ISBN 9789815058161

Typeset in Garamond by MAP Systems, Bangalore, India

www.penguin.sg

Contents

Introduction	vii
The Mayor	1
Three Dead Chickens	11
My Lovely Skull	21
Waiting For You	32
Room 511	43
The Elevator Game	58
Cathedraphobia	69
Baby Dream	82
The Garden	98
No Ordinary Day	114
Administrator Number One	130
Karaoke Nightmare	147
The Festival	163
Moongate	181
Water Flows Deepest	200

Introduction

'She started back, then again advanced, shuddered as she took up the skeleton hand . . .'

—Anne Radcliffe, *The Mysteries of Udolpho*

'Hold tight. We are going into a number of dark places . . .'

—Stephen King, *Skeleton Crew*

So what skeletons hide in your cupboard?

What secrets, dark memories are lodged in your skull?

I have a few.

I turn them into stories.

What do you do with yours?

Some people pretend they have none, but I know they do. We all have them for we all have memories, don't we? Not all of them good. Some most disturbing.

The bad ones we talk about, usually not to friends but to a psychiatrist. Or we keep them as brooding secrets.

Once, while in bed, a gecko fell on me. That's right, without warning, even as I dreamt of whatever I normally dream about. Yelling out in fear and disgust, I quickly brushed the slimy thing away. It fell on the floor and darted away.

Not an unexpected occurrence.

It was going to happen sooner or later. You see, I lived in a tiny cottage where a thriving family of perhaps twenty or more geckos scurried up walls, darted around drying crockery, hid behind the rice cooker. With their large bulbous eyes fixed on mine, we tried hard to ignore each other.

I took this disturbing memory of my night visitor and held it close like a lover. It was no big deal but nor was it something I was willing to share with friends or relatives over dinner. Keeping it secret, the memory would ferment and grow.

A secret that eventually morphed into 'Administrator Number One'. It's one of the fifteen dark stories you'll find in this collection. The ones in the story aren't your normal everyday geckos though, these reptiles like to kill.

As I write this, I'm living in an apartment block in Penang. I've counted only three geckos, so nothing to write home about. Gazing out of the window, I'm lucky enough to have a close sea-view and I can hear waves washing on the shore. An old couple are walking their two poodles on the esplanade in the searing midday heat.

Things people do for their dogs, right?

Which brings me to 'The Festival'. That story is no fun day out for pooches, nor one that will get their tales wagging with prizes and ribbons to be won at the dog show.

Not at all for, you see, it's a dog-eating festival. Most disgusting, I agree, but you didn't come here for ice-cream and roses, did you?

A lot of these stories come from walking.

They were inspired, brewed and came to life by frequent strolls, hikes and ambles on the island. In this I, hopefully, follow the footsteps of many writing luminaries whose long strolls formed an essential part of their creativity. I just hope I don't stumble and fall trying to mimic them!

Sometimes I find myself hiking up the Moongate trail near the Botanical Gardens. The uphill jungle track inspired the story of the same name. Then there's the jungly suburb of Pearl Hill where I once heard an uncanny cry echoing from high in the trees. The animal sounded like a child or a baby and so the idea emerged for 'Baby Dream'. I once also spied a beautiful banana grove there and from it sprouted the story 'Waiting for You'.

Not far from my apartment block, I came across an abandoned house with a dark overgrown garden, almost like a haunted forest in the middle of suburbia. I was captivated but no story emerged. Then, one day, quite by chance, I spied an old woman in rags sitting outside the house, piles of rubbish beside her. From this setting grew 'The Garden'.

A couple of years back, my story 'Three Dead Chickens' was published in *Horror Without Borders,* a world-wide flash fiction anthology. As we should always treat sustainability and recycling seriously, even if it's only for the sole purpose of inane marketing, I reused the body parts and expanded my 500-word tale into a new dark-comedic one. Another story, written in that same tongue-in-cheek vein is 'Karaoke Nightmare', inspired by one of my out-of-tune singing sessions.

Ideas, you see, can come from anywhere. They come from secrets, they come from walks. They can come from all events, all places, all people. We just need to be open to them.

I hope you enjoy these stories as I much as I enjoyed writing them.

Your friend in darkness,

Tunku Halim
23 August 2022

The Mayor

Tom pointed the Mauser M18 at him.

'Killing me is a dumb thing to do,' the Mayor hissed.

'Why?' Tom said. 'I've already killed your two bodyguards.'

When the two burly men in combat fatigues had spotted Tom trailing them, they hid amongst the rocks and trees and tried to ambush him, while their boss fled up the mountain.

'I'm a better shot than your lousy bodyguards, Mayor. You need to improve your hiring skills.'

The Mayor pulled off his hunting hat, spat at the dirt and wiped his large mouth with his sleeve.

'I've been the mayor for twenty years. So I hire and fire whoever I bloody well like!'

Tom shoved the barrel of the gun at his face. 'You stayed in power because you paid off everyone. Well, we've had enough of your bribery, fraud, blackmail . . . even bloody murder!'

The Mayor laughed. 'Murder? Not murder . . . I won't admit to that. But true, I paid off everyone, from beggars to tycoons. Everyone does that to stay in power.'

'That's bullshit, Mayor. It doesn't have to be that way. You were elected to serve the people. Or did you somehow forget that?'

The Mayor chuckled despite the gun in his face. 'I always knew you were the best of the lot, Tom. So honest and resilient the way you run that dry goods shop of yours with your beautiful wife. So you think killing me is going to end it, huh?'

1

'Well, it's a bloody start.'

'Oh, you're one clever man, trailing me up here when all your fellow citizens are hunting for me below, after their drunken celebrations.'

The Mayor, narrow eyes gleaming, gestured towards the town at the foot of the mountain, the pretty white buildings burnt orange by the setting sun. It was an isolated place where everyone poked their noses into each other's lives.

'I knew you'd hide up here where nobody comes,' Tom said. 'People are afraid of this mountain and its ancient forest because of those stories. Especially that monastery up there.'

He glanced at the stone ruins sitting at the top of the mountain, just beyond the tree line. For some unknown reason, it had been abandoned two hundred years ago. There were stories of devil worship, of monks found beheaded, their treasured library of illuminated books burnt to ashes. Just seeing its grey, crumbling walls like a crouching mythical stone beast filled Tom with cold dread.

The Mayor chortled. It was a harsh, spite-filled laughter.

'Those stories are all bullshit. To scare kids from coming up here. Look, let's talk. Why don't you get that gun out of my face?'

Tom hesitated. Then he lowered the gun and pointed it at the Mayor's stomach. 'So you thought no one would come up here because of those stories?'

'That's right, Tom. I was going to camp here for a week or so until things died down. You can understand that, can't you? Now that you killed my bodyguards, I'm going to need a new one, someone who's pretty handy with a gun, like yourself.'

'I'm not going to be your damn bodyguard!'

'Hey, I'm still the Mayor here and I could use someone like yourself. I should have won those damn elections . . .'

He rambled on about how victory should have been his, about how he had done so much for the town, about how ungrateful the citizens were. All the while his voice grew louder and more strident as it overflowed with self-righteousness.

'Hey, you can put that gun away,' he finally said, large mouth smirking. 'Let's do a deal. I have millions stashed away. I'll share several with you. How old are those boys of yours?'

'Ten and eight.'

'Well, they'll never need to work again. You can send them to the best colleges, buy them houses, set them up for life. And what about that beautiful wife of yours? You can buy her diamonds, jewels, fabulous presents anything she wants? So, go on, my friend, use your damn brains.'

Tom thought of that beachside cottage they had always wanted to buy. It was now within reach. He just had to say *yes*.

'Say *yes* to my generous offer, Tom,' the Mayor said, as if he could mind-read. 'This is an opportunity that only comes once in a lifetime.' His voice had turned soft, smooth and soothing. 'You could even be my right-hand man one day, the guy who gets things done. Because you're smart, so very capable and . . .'

He reached out to touch Tom's shoulder.

Tom stepped back. 'Shut up! I've got to think.'

His breath was heavy.

It was true, this was a lifetime's opportunity. He worked so damn hard just to get by. He lived for his family, he wanted the best for them. Now they could have everything.

'Go on, Tom,' the Mayor said in that same soothing voice. 'Just say *yes*. That's not so hard.'

But it was hard. Tom felt himself being torn in two directions. His fingers were trembling. A bead of sweat dripped down the side of his face. His grip loosened on the rifle.

'I don't know,' he whispered.

'Yes, you do, Tom,' the Mayor said, eyes gleaming. 'Of course, you do. Just say *yes* to me. Come on, my friend.'

Once again, he reached out to touch Tom's shoulder.

Tom stumbled back.

The Mayor stepped forward, a wide grin on his face.

Tom blinked. He had almost fallen in a moment of weakness, in a seduction that corrupts. It was a test of character, a test of will.

'No,' he whispered, shaking his head. 'Then I'll just be like you.'

'What's so bad about that, my friend? I can give you everything you . . .'

Tom pulled the trigger.

The Mayor's stomach exploded in a burst of blood and guts.

He stood, eyes wide, in mid-sentence then collapsed to his knees before keeling over, raising a cloud of dust.

This wasn't the first time that Tom had killed a man. He'd been in the army in a conflict zone. A wasted effort, billions spent and countless lives lost, but weren't they all? He decided that killing the Mayor was the best thing he'd ever done with a single bullet.

He contemplated leaving the body there but Tom had too much respect for the dead. So he pulled out the shovel from the Mayor's backpack and began digging.

By the time he had buried the Mayor in a shallow grave, night had fallen. He decided against tracking back to town in the dark and so pulled out the Mayor's tent and some provisions and set up for the night. He lit a campfire and made a simple meal.

So I've killed him. Tom thought.

But he wasn't going to let it bother him much. Their town was now safe from the Mayor and his evil corruption.

'Killing him was the right thing to do,' Tom whispered, running his hands over his face. 'No doubt about it.'

But still he doubted it and he pushed the thought aside. What was done was done.

He gazed at the moon and stars, smelt the freshness of the trees, heard owls hooting and felt a light breeze on his face.

He found a small whiskey bottle in the backpack and, finding solace by drinking most of it, watched the dome of stars, his thoughts on how they could build a better, free society now that the Mayor was dead.

It can happen, he thought. It's not just a dream.

As it was a warm night, he pulled out a ground sheet from the tent and got comfortable in the open. He spied a meteor hurling through the night sky before he dozed off.

He dreamt of the Mayor crouching over him, eyes wide, a grin on his blood-splattered face, a dagger raised in one hand and the gloating full moon above.

You're going to pay, whispered the Mayor. *Pay so very dearly.*

Then he was gone and in his place were his wife and two sons. She was weeping, strands of long hair over her cheeks, and his boys, dressed in pyjamas, were clutching onto her, bodies trembling.

Get away, Tom, she whispered, through her tears. *Run away from here!*

He stirred . . . for there was something else.

A sound. A low groaning noise that seemed to come from the soil beneath him.

He opened his eyes.

He listened again but all had gone quiet. The forest was hushed as though waiting for something, perhaps afraid of what might come.

In that chilling silence, he heard it again.

At first he thought it was just the wind. But as he listened, he realized it was a moaning from far away. As he got up to look, the sound drew closer, closer still and soon seemed to rise up from the soil around him.

He shivered. His throat dry.

The groaning sounded so tortured, so unearthly that it was no sound a living creature could make.

Feeling woozy from the whiskey, he peered warily through the shadowed trees.

Dim moonlight slanted in through the forest. Nothing moved.

Then he lifted his gaze to the ruined monastery. It sat there like a monstrous beast, still, unmoving, ready to pounce. Within its shadows, he glimpsed a shifting. At first he thought they were nothing but clouds lit by a silvery moon glow but, as the mass of white began to climb the walls and roll down the mountainside towards him, he realized it was a bank of fog.

Approaching quickly like a ghost army.

Of decapitated monks.

His face went cold.

For now there were many voices. Moaning.

The fog came rushing in through the trees.

Rolling over soil, fallen leaves, undergrowth and roots, swamping over his shoes and ankles, up to his knees.

The chanting was now deafening though he couldn't understand a word.

Sweat dripped from his brow despite the drop in temperature.

He smelt death. A sickly sweetness that dripped with blood.

Then the voices fell silent.

There came another sound.

A scratching, followed by a rhythmic thudding.

Like someone digging.

He swallowed and his eyes turned to the recently-dug grave.

Soil sprayed from it in small bursts.

Clumps of dirt flew out.

The moon glow revealed the abomination.

Fingers . . . hands . . . arms.

Pushing out.

A head emerged.

The body clambered out, soil falling off the shoulders, as the corpse dragged itself from the earth.

Tom's mouth fell open, heart pounding.

Beneath the grim moonlight, the Mayor got to his knees and slowly, ever so slowly, stood up, a grin like a leech on his pale face.

Fog swirled about the corpse's knees as if in league with this evil resurrection.

The corpse brushed dirt off its body. Then it staggered forward.

A clutch of worms wriggled out of dead sightless eyes. One crawled out of one nostril and back into the other. The nose half falling off the face.

The clothes were in tatters. The body so decomposed that it looked as though it had been buried for days rather than just hours.

It whiffed of rotting meat. Of horrid decay.

Tom felt nauseous, dizzy, not believing his eyes.

The Mayor licked his blackened teeth, several of which were missing. He spread his hands as if he was about to welcome his supporters at a political rally.

'So here I am, Tom,' the once-dead Mayor rasped. 'You see, you cannot kill me. Pestilence, corruption and evil can never die.'

Tom staggered back. 'W-What the hell? I-I killed you. I buried you!'

'Yes, you did indeed.' The Mayor wagged a rotting finger before Tom's face. 'But, guess what, my friend? I'm back.'

Tom jerked his head away. 'No! No! This can't be happening!'

'Oh yes it is, Tom. I knew the evil up here could help me. But I never guessed how powerful it would be. And now you are mine!'

Rotting fingers reached out, clawing the air with black fingernails.

The Mayor's laughter echoed like a raging wind around him.

Tom stumbled back, legs soft like jelly. 'Get away from me! Please!'

This couldn't be real. It had to be a nightmare. But nightmares didn't smell so bad. Nor did he ever dream of zombies.

Then he saw it on the mat beside the tent.

The Mauser!

Grabbing the rifle, he spun around, and dream or no dream, fired two shots into the Mayor.

One hit the chest. The other into the face, tearing out flesh, an eye, teeth and bits of worm.

The corpse lurched back under the impact. It groaned, stood still for a moment, before staggering forward, half-mouth turning into a grin, arms reaching, fingers claw-like.

Tom stumbled back, tripped over and fell on his back.

He screamed as the corpse leapt on him. He saw blinding, shrieking red as it bit into his throat ripping out blood, flesh and cartilage.

Tom's limbs quivered, then fell silent.

A warm wind blew down the mountainside.

Far away, a wolf howled.

'You should have accepted my offer,' hissed the Mayor. 'Your principles, your ideals, your integrity stands for nothing in this world.'

He laughed, got down on his haunches and ate Tom's flesh, blood dribbling like wine down its chin.

Having had his fill, he put on his hunting hat and strolled down the mountain, the fog bank following him.

Whispering.

With each step, his bullet-riddled, decomposed body began to rejuvenate himself.

As he reached the bottom of the mountain, the fog spilled over towards the three cemeteries on the edge of town. The dead, of whatever denomination or religion, whether buried yesterday or a century ago, no longer slumbered in peace, for the fog's ancient, unnatural, monastic forces nudged them awake.

There followed a commotion as soil sprayed upwards, clumps of earth thrown out, coffins splintered, tombstones knocked over as corpses eagerly pushed their way out of their graves.

Even as morning sunlight crept over the tops of the white buildings, the Mayor, fully rejuvenated, fresh and keenly alive, swaggered up the high street. Scores of the undead shuffled in behind him. Soon they too, from dusty skeletons to the freshly buried became living, breathing people.

Except they were not, for they were the undead.

'Decay, pestilence, corruption, evil lives on!' the Mayor bellowed, his voice echoing like thunder against the buildings. 'It is with me. With all of us. This town is ours again!'

His followers chanted. 'Ours again! Ours again! Ours again!'

The town bells rang and the alarmed citizens armed with clubs, guns and knives scrambled out to challenge this power seizure but were bloodied and beaten back for they were no match for the undead.

For such creatures knew not how to die.

Far up on the mountain's wooded slope, beside the forest, beneath the ruined monastery, Tom's half-eaten corpse lay on the blood-splattered mat, dead eyes staring as the sun made its unimpeded way across the sky.

Wolves, jackals and crows stayed away. Perhaps out of respect. Or perhaps because of the pestilence that had already half-feasted on him.

In the town square below, the bodies of Tom's wife and two sons, together with candidates who had won the elections or those known to oppose the Mayor's rule, were strung up in the town square, their bodies left to rot on the blood-stained walls.

The townspeople cowered in the shadows, afraid of even the sunlight, hardly believing this turn of events. As evening descended, they withdrew to their homes.

Worried and whispering. Waiting for a change that must surely inevitably come.

But would it ever?

In his palatial home, the Mayor threw a lavish barbecue for his new-found followers who boisterously chatted and chortled, not quite believing their stroke of luck and the riches that would be theirs. The Mayor stood triumphantly beside his brightly-lit swimming pool, cigar in one hand, whiskey in another, and grinned.

He had become mayor for life and, for him, life was never ending.

Three Dead Chickens

Three chickens are dead, necks broken.

One in the kitchen. Two in the living room.

Staring at the mangled carcasses, feathers strewn all over like the aftermath of a pillow fight, Loke can scarcely believe it.

He turns to his sister's horrified face. 'That confirms it, Fay. This place is bloody haunted.'

Fay's face is awfully pale. 'It smells terrible here. Like a meat section in the wet market.'

'When did you never go to a wet market? Anyway, it's a good thing uncle suggested we use the chickens!'

That's because when uncle's daughter, their cousin-sister, brought her baby along to see the single-storey bungalow devoid of furniture, the baby burst into unstoppable, unconsolable tears. Fay, on witnessing this distressing omen, was most alarmed.

The property agent, who was desperate for her sales commission, managed to get the owner's understandably reluctant permission, and so the cockerels were brought in last night.

And now the poor fowls were dead.

Fay shakes her head. 'No wonder they're selling this place so cheaply. Didn't even think it might be haunted. Now I know it is. I suppose we have to clean it all up now.'

She rubs one foot repeatedly against the white tiled floor as if trying to coax the house to clean itself up or, better still, to rid itself of this unwelcome haunting.

Loke scrutinizes the broken neck of one cockerel whose one eye stares back accusingly. He turns away and takes a sharp breath. 'It's an awful, ugly mess.'

After the run-down bungalow is cleaned up and the carcasses disposed of by their mother's Indonesian maid, they meet the agent beneath the dreary car porch, surrounded by an overgrown garden.

'Everything okay?' the agent asks, her smile though drops like a rock when she sees their scrunched-up faces.

Fay bites her lips. 'No, it's not good. I can't buy it. The chickens died. The house is haunted.'

The agent blinks. Once. Twice. Her mouth falls open. 'What?'

'The chooks had their necks broken,' Loke adds. 'This house has bad spirits. Only a fool would buy it.'

'No, that can't be right.' The agent rubs the back of her neck. 'The owner never had a problem before. Maybe the chickens were ill. You know, weak chickens. Caught a virus. Bird flu.'

Fay tries to hand the keys back. 'Sick cockerels don't end up with broken necks.'

The agent ignores the keys and whispers, 'You know, I spoke to the owner earlier. He says he can reduce the price by two hundred thousand.'

'What?' Fay exclaims. 'Two hundred thousand?'

'Yes, two hundred thousand.'

Fay turns to Loke. 'That's a big discount. Huge even. It's so cheap.'

Loke frowns. 'But, Fay, the place . . . it's bloody haunted.'

'But we can fix it, Loke. We can get someone to get rid of the ghost.' She grabs his arm, 'It's a real steal!'

* * *

So haunted or not, Fay who can't resist a bargain, whether a Parkson dress or an iPad keyboard, ends up buying the run-down single storey bungalow.

As soon as she collects the keys, she gets her mum's maid to clean up the house because, bad spirit or not, Fay is OCD about cleanliness.

Loke has a different kind of cleansing on his brain.

But, unlike booking a car ride or a food delivery, there isn't an app to book an exorcism. He remembers his friend, Vijay, though who has often mentioned a holy man and who would no doubt conduct such a pugnacious exercise. So he sends Vijay a message.

Sorry, my friend, Vijay replies. *The holy man has gone missing. Was last seen heading a group meditation in a cave. I'll keep asking around.*

Loke though has more luck with his sales colleague, Idrus, who had once mentioned using a *bomoh* to thwart a love spell on his sister.

'And she forgot that fat old guy just like that,' Idrus said proudly. 'Imagine, he wanted my sister as his third wife. She wanted to give up everything for him. Wanted to stop uni too. No way would my family allow that.'

'So this bomoh just got rid of the love spell?' Loke asked.

'Yep, just came once to the house. Blew smoke into her face and after that she didn't even want to even look at that dirty old man. That dirty bastard came to the house, but I just chased him away. Even threw stones at his car!'

So Loke called Idrus.

'I'll get the bomoh no problem,' Idrus says. 'I'll come too. I want to see him at work. He's really good!'

'Tomorrow night then?'

'No problem.'

So that night, they sit cross-legged on the living room floor. Fay glances at Loke warily, who eyes Idrus hopefully, who, in turn, nods at the bomoh encouragingly.

The shaman is in his fifties, overweight and unshaven. He wears a loose white headdress that resembles a napping cat, a faded sarong and a T-shirt telling them to Fly Emirates. From his dark, dark wrinkled face, he turns away from his phone and gives them a penetrating gaze.

'Leave the front door open,' he says in Malay, his breath smelling of cigarettes. 'So the bad spirits can flee this house after I give them a good, solid whacking.'

With lights off, he takes a flame to the charcoal burner which he pushes with one dark foot to the centre of the circle.

The flame throws shuddering shadows on their expectant faces as insect shrills echo through curling smoke.

Eyes closed, the bomoh begins his chant.

The flame in the charcoal burns brighter, flames sparking upwards like crazed fireflies.

Without warning, a cold wind like dirty fingers grasps their faces and a rotting black odour rises from the floor.

Loke belches, gags, one hand clamped over his mouth.

Still the shaman chants, louder and louder, cheeks quivering under the strain, eyes fluttering.

The bomoh suddenly goes silent, lips trembling like a fish caught on a hook, wide eyes fixed on the ceiling. His tongue flops out.

A sudden roar shakes the room.

The shaman jerks away and shields his terrified face with his hands. 'No, no, no, no. Why have you brought me here?'

'W-What's wrong?' Loke blurts in Malay, eyes wide in fright.

The bomoh gestures, hands trembling. 'The thing, the black cloud . . . it is an ancient evil, far too powerful for me. I cannot do this. I have not the strength . . .'

'What can we do?' Idrus gets up, gasping. 'Please tell us!'

The shaman shakes his head. 'Nothing. There's nothing you can do. And, oh, I cannot leave. I am trapped by its awful power. I should not have challenged it. If I try to leave, I will die.'

Loke stands up, his legs feeling like jelly. 'What? You'll die if you try to leave the house?'

The shaman nods. 'Leave me here. Maybe it will let me go in the morning. Or maybe you'll find me dead like a mangled dog. What will happen to me is Allah's will.'

Fay, heart pounding, turns to Idrus. 'We can't just let him be trapped here. We can't let him die!'

Loke turns to his sister, his eyes wild. 'No, we can't. This spirit is far too powerful. We need help.'

'So what are we going to do?'

Loke has pulled out his wallet and is counting cash. 'I was talking to a *daoshi* this morning,' he mutters. 'He was going to charge a lot of money, so that's why I didn't want to use him. But we have no choice now.'

So, foot tapping on the tiled floor, Loke makes the desperate call.

* * *

The daoshi arrives soon after.

Dressed in a loose white robe, the seventy-year-old Taoist monk steps into the house, his face so stern and powerful that Faye reckons he can easily defeat any hungry ghost, even one on an extended hunger strike.

'So, how can I help?' he asks in Hokkien as he flourishes his robe, flapping them bird-like.

Above his bushy white eyebrows, his bald head glows in the beseeching moonlight that streams in through the front door. A monk who can easily be mistaken for a wizened Shaolin master. Or perhaps vice versa.

Loke and Fay explain the situation.

The daoshi nods gravely and fingers his long white beard.

'Sounds like a powerful spirit. I have defeated many formidable ones and this will be no different.'

Smelling of Chinese herbs, he carefully arranges his robes and joins the circle, sitting opposite the bomoh.

The two men nod at each other and exchange a few words in Malay.

'Sounds bad,' says the daoshi, furrowing his white eyebrows.

The bomoh nods, his face scrunched up and weary. 'Yes, very bad, very, very bad.'

The monk lights several incense sticks and places them on a wooden holder. He eyes each person in the circle. 'Don't worry, dear friends, I will subdue this evil thing.'

With one finger, he traces mysterious symbols in the air. The flame from the charcoal burner lights up his determined face. With a shout, he leaps to his feet. He strikes out with his fists, blocking with his elbows while his tiger-claw fingers swipe through the smoky air.

Then grunting loudly, he stumbles back as if he has been kneed in the belly. His mouth falls open, his eyes dazed.

A chilling breeze hits them and there wafts that putrefying stench.

There's a thunderous roar and suddenly his legs are taken out from under him and he drops to the floor. He yells and grabs his injured bald head.

Loke and Idrus rush over to help the old man sit up.

'I forgot,' the daoshi gasps. His eyes dazed, one hand tugging at his beard. 'I have a dinner meeting now, full eight course dinner . . . oh no, no, I can't go. I . . . I am its prisoner here. I should never have tried to fight it.'

'What?' Loke cries, eyes bulging. 'You're its prisoner too?'

The monk slowly nods, now looking terribly old and fragile. 'This evil spirit . . . it's too formidable. Better kung fu too. Now I'm stuck here.'

Loke glances at Fay and Idrus, his stomach cold as ice. 'What the hell are we going to do now?'

Before either of them could answer him, Loke's phone chimes an EDM tune. He slips it out of his shorts and answers it.

'That was Vijay,' he says breathlessly, one hand running through his hair. 'I asked him earlier about getting a Hindu holy man. He said the guy was missing but now he's found him. They're coming over now.'

* * *

All eyes fall on the *saadhu* as he sweeps into the house.

Vijay, who is beaming brightly, follows and introduces the Hindu holy man.

The holy man is stick-thin, bare chested and wears a bright orange loin cloth with a garland of frangipanis around his neck. He has long unkempt greasy hair and has two bold white streaks down his forehead.

Eyes sparklingly bright, he takes his place in the circle. He smells of coriander and curry leaves. Vijay sits between the holy man and Loke.

'Finding him was very difficult,' Vijay mutters. 'For he just wanders around from place to place like a lost goat. But he is very powerful. Very holy.'

'I hope he's powerful enough,' Loke says. 'He's our only hope now.'

The saadhu smiles and puts his palms together as he greets them. Next he pulls out a set of wooden prayer beads and, eyes closed, begins to chant a holy mantra. His voice resonates as his naked hairy chest rises and falls. The flames from the charcoal burner throw misshapen shadows on his deeply wrinkled face as his voice rises mightily, brimming with all the holy power of the Ganges.

Without warning, a cold gust blows through them and that same vile stench seeps like poisonous miasma from the floor.

Fay gasps and clamps a hand over her mouth.

The saadhu's beads rattle loudly in his fingers, taking on a life of their own. His eyes fly open and the beads are flung across the room just as the garland of frangipanis are ripped from his neck and, without warning, his body is thrown against the wall and he collapses like a corpse to the floor.

White petals uselessly drift down like confetti at an extravagant birthday party.

Loke, Idrus and Vijay scurry over to help him up.

Scraps of flowers are scattered in his long hair, several poke from a corner of his mouth. He coughs them out in a spray of white. He makes a guttural noise, wipes his cracked lips with a shaky hand and whispers to Vijay.

Vijay turns to the group. Alarm grips his face.

'He said this evil spirit is far too powerful for him. That he is now trapped here. If he tries to leave . . .'

'He will die.' Fay says, ending the sentence for him.

'What are we going to do?' Loke moans, one hand desperately massaging his temple.

Fay shakes her head. 'The three holy men have failed. The bomoh, the daoshi and the saadhu.'

Loke frowns at Idrus and Vijay who are deep in conversation.

'What are you two talking about?'

'We were just saying that we need to do this together,' Idrus says.

'Yes,' Vijay adds. 'Doing things on our own isn't going to work. We'll be much stronger if we're united.'

Loke's eyes widen. 'No matter what race or religion?'

'Yes, of course!' Fay says. 'We must work together! As a family!'

* * *

Everyone in the circle are holding hands, the bomoh, the daoshi, the saadhu together with Fay, Loke, Idrus and Vijay.

'What do we do now?' Fay asks.

'Don't know,' Loke replies. 'Just close our eyes, I suppose.'

Eyes shut, hands grasping hands, it doesn't take long for them to feel a tingling like beetles crawling on their arms.

Then the three holy men begin to chant, each in their own tongue, with their own holy words, warbling voices rising and falling in different pitches but, strangely, begin to harmonize. The tingling now becomes a surging force like a powerful breeze through trees which grows stronger and stronger into a potent summoning.

A silent irresistible call deep into the night.

But what is being summoned?

As the flame in the centre of the circle dims, there's a rustling in the garden followed by a clinking on the tiled floor as something or *somethings* enter the house.

Fay opens her eyes and sees them.

Three chickens!

They strut into the house assertively, even majestically, with the moon shining brightly like a holy halo behind them. The cockerels, misty-looking and glowing, squawk as they flap their wings into the circle.

With smoke drifting over them, they strut around the charcoal burner, making clucking noises, cocking their heads as they eye the human audience around the circle.

Fay gasps.

For now they leap up in different directions.

One chicken is poised on the bomoh's head, another perches on the *daoshi's* skull and yet another prances on the saadhu's.

The fowls crane their necks to give the gawking humans a reproaching look. Then they turn their beaks upwards and, wings beating, begin to loudly crow.

Loke can hardly breathe as a smoky mass spills from the ceiling. It is surrounded by a multitude of long, snake-like arms and within the smog are bulging greedy golden eyes brimming with . . .

Evil, murder and corruption.

The crowing, this harmony of the three birds, is so cacophonous that he covers his ears. Sweat drips from his brow. The blackness stinks beyond horrible.

As the cockerels continue to powerfully bellow, the smog pulls back. Pulsing and quivering as it shrinks smaller and smaller even as the crowing turns so thunderous that it is surely beyond hearing.

The black mass is no more than the size of a gym ball, then a soccer ball and, finally, a ping pong ball and then, with a faint popping sound, it vanishes into oblivion.

Loke can breathe again.

Everyone stares at each other.

'It's gone,' Fay whispers. 'The horrible smell, it's gone. The room, the house, it feels so much lighter too.'

'The chickens . . . they've disappeared too,' Loke says, turning to the vacant heads of the holy men who are now nodding gravely.

'Those dead chooks saved us,' Fay sighs. 'The poor, poor things with their necks all broken.'

'Yes, saved us they did,' Loke said. 'But nothing to be sad about.'

'Oh, why not?'

'Chickens. Well, they die all the time, don't they, Fay?'

'Yes, of course, they do.'

The group staggers up from the circle and, grinning and whispering, they depart the once haunted house for a scrumptious dinner.

But no one dares order chicken.

My Lovely Skull

'Where the hell did you get that?'

I grinned at Farhan. He was shocked as I expected.

We sat on the floor in his bedroom in a bungalow he lived with his parents. It had just turned dark outside and insect noises crept in through large windows.

Farhan scratched his head. 'Is it real?'

'Yes,' I said, grinning. 'Of course, it is.'

'Where the heck did you find it?'

So I told him about my beach walk.

Ibu had sent me there to gather shellfish for dinner because the waves had been enormous the day before, pounding the beaches powerfully. We could even hear them from our low-cost flat which was some distance away.

Wild waves had churned up the seabed and washed huge amounts of debris onto the beach, including lots of fresh shellfish. When I arrived that evening, there were several others, old Indian couples and young Chinese girls with their mothers, harvesting them from the sand and filling up their plastic bags. The carpet of shells on the sand made clicking sounds as waves, now calmed down, washed over them.

I had just picked a few green mussels when my slipper hit something buried in the sand beside a discarded plastic bottle. I doubted it was a rock as it wasn't so hard. Nor was it a ball. Hoping it was something valuable, I squatted and dug around it with my hands.

21

When I realized what I'd found, I gasped and fell back, my bottom upon the wet sand and stared, hardly believing my eyes.

The eye sockets glowered at me . . . in the gleaming pinkish glow of sunset.

I gingerly placed a finger on the top of the skull. It felt warm. Perhaps it was from the heat of the day. Or perhaps the flesh, only recently living, had been hewn from it.

No, that's crazy thinking.

I jerked my hand away, but not before feeling, a tingling going up my arm. But that, of course, had to be my imagination.

Yet, as my eyes were fixed on the skull, it stared back . . . right through me. My chest quivered as I beheld the shadowed hollows of the eye sockets. At the smooth sand-speckled cranium. At the row of teeth whiter than sand.

Even with the skull still half-buried, I knew that it had to be mine. It would be my prized possession. Mine and no-one else's.

So I hastily emptied my small collection of mussels from the plastic bag, pulled some seaweed from the mouth and began to push the skull into it.

But instead of slipping into the bag, the skull rolled down the sand towards the sea as if trying to flee. As if the thing had a life of its own.

Which it once did!

I tried to stop it with my slippered foot but it tumbled away into the water. I thought I had lost my prize but then, to my relief, a large wave pushed it back up onto the beach.

Yes! Got you!

I fell on my knees and grabbed it, water splashing on my T-shirt.

I glanced around to see if anyone else had spotted the rolling skull but they were too busy gathering shellfish.

I hurriedly pushed the skull into the plastic bag.

'There's no escaping,' I whispered. 'You're mine!'

The thought of owning the skull, sent a thrill to me. I would proudly show it to all my friends. Some, especially the girls, would be terrified, others would think that I was the coolest guy around. Imagine me, owning a scary skull!

It was an amazing find. But it was just a skull, right? No big deal. But I didn't know of anyone else who possessed one.

Farhan, my best friend, would go absolutely crazy over it. I quickly messaged him, telling him that I was coming over. Next, I messaged Ibu, fibbing that there wasn't much shellfish and that I was going to Farhan's for dinner.

I picked up the plastic bag and was surprised at how heavy it was. Worried that the bag might rip apart, I cradled it in my arms, strolling with my new acquisition close against my heart.

So there we were, both sitting cross-legged on the floor of Farhan's big bedroom, a widescreen TV on one wall, an Apple laptop on his desk playing a Hip-Hop playlist, our eyes transfixed on the skull that seemed to intelligently scrutinize us.

'So you found it on the beach?' Farhan continued to stare wide-eyed, his curly hair falling over his forehead. He wore shiny shorts and a Nike T-shirt. He owned lots of designer stuff which he no doubt proudly wore at that expensive private university he went to.

But he doesn't own a skull!

I proudly stroked the pale cranium, feeling that warmth tingling beneath my fingers. 'Sure I did. Can't you see from the sand?'

Farhan swallowed. 'Oh yeah, you've messed up my floor.'

'We can wipe it up later,' I said with a smirk. Farhan could pretend to fuss over his floor but he was obviously jealous of my find.

Farhan eyes narrowed. 'I've never seen a real skull before. Maybe at a museum. But not like this. How did it get on the beach?'

I shrugged. 'Don't know. The rough seas must have dragged it up from the bottom.'

'Do you think it's old? Or did someone recently get killed or drowned or got eaten by sharks?'

I ignored him and continued to stroke the top of my skull, my fingers warm.

Farhan frowned. 'Maybe we should call the police. Maybe this person was murdered?'

'What will they do?'

He blinked. 'Don't know. But what are you going to do with it?'

'I'm going to keep it. Might be valuable.'

Farhan chuckled. 'Nah, it's just a stupid skull.'

'It's not stupid! You're damn stupid!'

I couldn't understand why I said that. Or why my blood suddenly boiled.

I was about to say sorry when my eyes latched onto the skull's eye sockets. Their hollow shadows leapt into my startled eyes and, for a moment, I thought I heard the white row of teeth rattle as if it was trying to speak.

Then it *did* talk . . . in a young woman's voice.

He has no right to call me stupid!

'What the hell . . .' I whispered.

I turned to see if Farhan had heard the skull speak but a thick mist had fallen over his face and it shrouded the entire room in a cold, swirling grey. The music was gone. All I could see, all I could hear was the skull.

He thinks you're stupid too!

I stared at it, unbelievingly.

Don't you agree?

'H-He always has,' I stammered back. 'He got better grades in all the school exams.'

Thinks he's so rich. He's always looked down at you and your family.

I slowly nodded.

She was damn right. Why didn't I realize it before?

So what if we lived in low-cost flat? He had no right to look down on us. And he got better grades because his family could afford a personal tutor. We struggled just to pay for schoolbooks.

'How dare he call me stupid!'

She whispered in a delicate, soothing voice:

Now you know the truth. Your best friend is no real friend.

I sprang to my feet, eyes blazing at Farhan. The grey mist had vanished and I saw him clearly, more clearly than ever before.

He was babbling something in protest, bewilderment in his face, hair falling stupidly over his forehead, but I heard not a word. There was nothing he could say that would change anything. My skull had told me the truth.

'In all the years I've know you,' I hissed, 'how come you've never come to visit me?'

He raised his hands in protest. 'W-What do you mean? I always thought you preferred to come here, to my house.'

I pointed a finger at him. 'No, no, no! You think my family is beneath you, don't you? Think you're too rich, too good to visit us, eh?'

His face trembled. 'That's not true, I never . . .'

'Can't stand the smell of rubbish spilling over from our big bins? Can't climb our dark dingy staircase? Don't want to see our noisy neighbours living in cramped-up flats, their kids dressed in rags?'

Something incomprehensible gurgled up from Farhan's throat but I didn't hear him for my boiling blood drowned out the sound and sense of everything. It surged into my head like wild waves pounding the beach.

This so-called friendship had to end.

I spun to glance around the room. The big TV. The Apple lap-top playing music, Hip-Hop that now seemed so horrible. Textbooks and messy papers on his desk.

A pair of scissors gleamed.

Yes, that was it. It would cut all ties. End his fucking life.

I dashed over and grabbed it.

Turned and leapt.

His mouth dropped open as he fell back.

I jammed it hard into his neck.

He shrieked in surprise and pain. But I didn't care.

Once, twice, three times, I viciously stabbed.

Blood splattered on the floor. On his bed. All over my clothes.

When I had finished, I grinned at the scissors, dripping with blood.

He deserved it.

His parents were thankfully out for they would have heard the commotion.

As I had the house to myself, I took my time to cut and slice his neck until Farhan was almost decapitated. I chuckled at the thought that I could chuck his severed head into the sea so that it would decompose into a skull for some other lucky person to find.

Then . . . all of a sudden, in my blood-soaked clothes . . . I felt as if I'd woken from an awful, awful nightmare. I stared at his mutilated, bloodied body. I gasped and dropped the scissors. It clattered to the floor.

'No, no, no,' I whispered. 'What the hell have I done?'

I dropped to my knees, my eyes fixed unbelievingly at Farhan's mutilated, bloodied body. It felt as though the earth would open and swallow me up, devour me in its anger.

'W-Why did I kill you!' I moaned, pressing my fingers so deep into my skull so that it felt as though it might explode.

Tears streamed down my cheeks.

Then I heard the young woman, whispering. It was soothing like beautiful music echoing deep in my head.

Oh, don't cry, my dear. Don't you cry, my darling.

My breath spilled out. I felt the horror of what I'd done slip away. I felt I could breathe again.

I turned to gaze at the pale object on the floor. The skull, which I'd almost forgotten was there. It sat, so innocently, so alone, yet glowing magically in the semi-darkness.

You did the right thing. It whispered in that beautiful, calming voice.

He deserved to die. He would have become your worst enemy.

I clambered on all fours towards the skull. 'Is . . . is that really true?'

Of course. He can't call you stupid anymore. Can't look down at your family.

'Yes, yes . . . I know you're right. But I . . . .'

You're got blood all over yourself. I don't like being so sandy either. We need a shower.

I picked up my skull and cradled her in my arms. 'Yes . . . yes, of course. A wonderful idea.'

I wandered into Farhan's bathroom and allowed water to spray like a soothing waterfall over the two of us.

You did a good job, she said, grinning at me.

I rocked her in my arms like a baby.

'Farhan had this nice bathroom all to himself. So big too! How come some people are just so lucky?'

Oh, don't think about that, my dear. Think about us here, right now.

She said it in a soft, seductive voice.

What did she mean? *Think about us here, right now.*

I stared into the hollows of her eye sockets, water splashing on us.

Us.

We were a couple.

Of course.

I understood what she meant.

She was mine and I was hers. We belonged together.

I felt my body quiver with excitement.

I brought my lips to her mouth. My tongue slipping sensuously over her teeth.

A flurry of lights burst in my head. I could hardly breathe. My heart pounding.

I felt a hardening below.

So I reached it and stroked myself.

I gasped as I ejaculated into her mouth.

Drying us both off with Farhan's fluffy towel, I slipped on some clothes I found in his wardrobe.

Now we have to get rid of the evidence.

I did as she asked and set fire to the house.

* * *

I strolled back towards our low-cost flat.

I never owned a genuine Nike t-shirt and I liked the way the material felt on my body.

Just Do It.

Indeed I did. Killed Farhan just like that. Without thinking.

Just Did It.

But what pleased me more was carrying his Adidas backpack. I wore it over my chest, so that she was pressed against me, close against my beating heart. Once, I gave into the temptation of unzipping the backpack to gaze into her eye sockets beneath the moonlight while, in the distance, flames danced behind us.

Soon I reached our building, a decaying dwarf sitting beneath the surrounding soaring condominiums where the wealthy dwelt. But I didn't care. I had all I needed.

Chickens darted away as I strolled into the compound, past haphazardly parked motorcycles, abandoned supermarket trolleys, pools of stagnant water and stinking drains. I climbed four levels, up the grimy staircase. I wandered down the open corridor past other flats, clothes drying on the balcony rails. Cooking smells and video noises spilled from louvered windows.

I stepped into our dingy home.

Ayah was in his sarong, smoking and watching TV. He grunted when he saw me. Ibu was in the kitchen.

'So no shellfish today?' she asked.

'None,' I replied.

'Maybe you should go earlier next time.'

I said I would and went to my bedroom which I shared with my fifteen-year-old brother. He was in bed playing with his phone.

'Hey, got a new bag?' he asked.

'Nah, Farhan lent it to me.'

'New clothes too?'

'I borrowed them.'

'Nice,' he said, eyes sucked back into his phone.

I took the bag off, placed it on my rickety bed and went to the bathroom.

When I got back, I found my brother staring into the bag.

He turned to me, blinking hard. 'Where the hell did you get that?'

I pushed him away. 'None of your business.'

He grabbed my shoulder. 'Just tell me where you got it? I won't tell anyone.'

I glared at him. 'On the beach. I found her on the beach.'

'Her? How do you know it's a woman?'

'I just know,' I hissed. 'Now leave me alone!'

We didn't speak for the rest of the evening and, when I switched off the light, I secretly removed the skull from the bag and pulled her close to me beneath the thin blanket.

'Good night,' my brother said.

'Yeah, sleep well,' I mumbled.

I lay awake with her nestled against my warm beating heart. My brother was softly breathing. Even though the ceiling fan was on, it was warm and perspiration trickled down my neck.

She whispered to me about her life in a beautiful mansion filled with antiques and heirlooms. About how she would sit at her walnut dressing table by the window every evening and how her faithful servant would brush her long hair as she watched the evening light spill over distant mountains.

About how she was on a ship, with the largest sails she had ever seen, journeying to her arranged wedding in a distant land. But then, on the second day, they were attacked by pirates. Their precious goods and jewels plundered and they were all thrown into the turbulent sea.

Whether it was last year or a hundred years ago, I didn't know. Tears though streamed down my cheeks.

She told me not to cry and so we kissed. My lips slipping against her rows of teeth, my body quivering.

So gorgeous, so lovely, she must have been. Her skin, smooth and soft, her face pale and beautiful, her long tresses of hair flowing down her bare shoulders to her breasts. I imagined us making love, she on top of me and softly moaning.

Then she whispered.

Your brother wants to steal me. Wants me all to himself.

'I know that,' I whispered back. 'I saw it in his greedy eyes.'

He'll steal me when you're not looking, my dear.

I nodded.

Are you going to let him, my darling?

I crept over to my brother's bed and knelt over his sleeping body. He was breathing deeply, his body hardly stirring at my presence, at the creaking of his bed.

'Nobody will take her away from me,' I whispered, as I stared at his curled-up figure. 'Not even you.'

My hands grabbed his throat.

His eyes flew open.

He tried to scream but only a gurgling emerged.

He struggled, legs kicking, hands hitting out, but I was much stronger than him. I squeezed harder and harder, sweat dripping down my forehead as I stared into his wild, frightened eyes. Finally, his limbs weakly struck at my shoulders before they dropped to the mattress.

The was nothing left for me to do but steal Ayah's motorcycle.

I crept out of the flat, along the corridor and down the stairs. We shot down the dark road in the early hours of morning, beneath the blur of streetlights, the glow of the moon above, cool wind in my face, Adidas bag strapped securely to my front.

She was close against my heart as always, sighing with happiness.

I was grinning joyfully.

Free and in love!

After riding past several towns, I stopped at a convenience store for coffee. It would be a long journey and my journey, with the love of my life, was just beginning.

As I sat on the motorcycle, eyeing the passing people and vehicles going through their humdrum day, I realized that in life people will do what they can to steal from you, so never give them a chance.

You must kill them.

So if we ever cross paths and if I see your greedy eyes yearning to steal my lovely skull, then I will follow you and slice up your throat. That I can promise you.

I've done it once and I'll gladly, oh so gladly, do it again.

Just you watch.

Waiting For You

She slipped the knife into the reusable shopping bag that said 'This Bag Saves the World'. Herman, her Golden Retriever, pulled on the leash, tongue lolling, joyful to be going out at last.

It was after six in the evening and she had abandoned her usual morning walk because of the plumber. These workmen were always late. It was frustrating and she had wasted a whole morning waiting. When he finally arrived and the work done, fixtures replaced, spanners put away, it had gotten too hot.

So here she was on an evening walk to replace the morning one.

She had spied the stand of banana trees just yesterday morning when the air was cool and dew lingered on the windows and windshields of parked cars. Passing a troop of white-faced, long-tailed monkeys frolicking on an electrical cable beside a house with a big red altar at the front gate, she took a turn and strolled down a steep road which she never took as it led to a dead end. But for some inexplicable reason, she followed it and as the steep road curved, the stand of banana trees beside a wall, stained black by rain, met her eyes.

It was perfectly composed, like a painting, amongst several houses. The elongated sun-drenched leaves swayed in the barest breeze. The stand of graceful trees seemed out of place amongst the weed-infested verges covered in dead leaves, dog and monkey shit fouling the road, tangled vines on the overhead electrical cables and jungle embracing it all.

The bananas hung heavily, two green bunches bright and inviting. Being so large, she surmised that they were perhaps plantains. This was public land and she had as much right to harvest them as anybody else, didn't she?

'Come let's take a look,' she said to Herman.

But Herman whined and pulled away, tugging on the leash. He sat recalcitrantly on the road and refused to budge.

Herman whimpered as if petrified, as if warning her not to take another step. That something dangerous waited in the banana grove.

'You're being silly, Herman,' she said, although a part of her felt that her dog knew more than she did. For she momentarily felt that there was something else in the grove other than the hanging fruit. Something not entirely wholesome.

She glared at Herman, for making her feel this way. 'Come on, let's go home then. We'll come back tomorrow. I'll bring a knife to cut down the bananas.'

So now, in the evening light, she strolled down the steep dead-end road to the banana grove, hoping the fruits would still be there.

'Must be back by seven,' she whispered to Herman. 'That's when he'll be back from the office.'

Thinking of her husband, she clutched her injured left shoulder which had struck the dining table after he shoved her.

'Bitch,' he had growled, face hard and crimson. 'Damn bloody bitch!'

His voice was different, as if the words were glued together, like it always was after drinking.

Then he spun her around, punched her in the stomach and shoved her to the kitchen floor.

He never hit her in the face though. Didn't want anyone to know.

And she never fought back. For it made it ten times worse.

'I'm so so sorry,' he had said the next morning when he found her curled up on the sofa were she had spent the night. 'I don't know what came over me. It won't happen again. It's . . . it's the damn drink. But I'm going to stop. Believe me, I will.'

She stared silently at him.

That evening, after work, he had brought a bouquet of roses. 'For you, baby,' he said. 'You mean everything to me.'

She took them and sobbed. It made it so much harder to bear.

The last time he had brought perfume. The time before that was chocolates, that was after he'd almost broken her arm.

His gifts, his apologies, his sweet words they amounted to nothing.

After their lavish hotel wedding, all had been good that first three months.

They would visit friends and relatives, stroll around the neighbourhood, holding hands, smiling and laughing. Ate at nice restaurants and went shopping.

'Marital bliss,' she had said to herself, smiling at the mirror as she put on lipstick. 'Now I know what it is.'

But a week later, he came home with whiskey on his breath. The bedroom door was flung open and a stranger entered.

'What the hell do you do here all day!' he hissed, yanking off his tie and dragging her off the bed.

As she lay bewildered on the parquet floor, she saw the twisted expression, the welling darkness, madness in his eyes.

Then the beatings started.

She was too ashamed to tell anyone but kept telling herself to leave, but somehow it never happened, and, without realizing it, four years had passed.

She never knew when the beatings would start. He often worked late at the office so she never knew when he would stop at a bar on the way home. Then he would climb the stairs, breath stinking, eyes narrowing, fists clenched. It was not just the violence but the uncertainty that drove her despair. She felt like drowning herself.

Once, after an ugly beating, she crawled to the bathroom and, to her horror, saw blood trickling down her thighs.

'Oh God,' she had whispered as she clutched her stomach.

She called the ambulance herself. But it was too late. She had miscarried.

After that she secretly had an IUD inserted for she decided that no baby was going to be brought into this nightmare.

Shaking her head at the memories, she blinked away a tear. These walks were her sole refuge, letting her slip away from the house, from his domain, where she could forget about him. For that hour or so, she no longer felt imprisoned as she strolled past houses surrounded by jungle or was it a jungle surrounded by houses? She could never decide.

When she reached the banana grove, dusk had strangely fallen earlier than usual and shadows ran deep.

Once again, Herman pulled away against the leash, whining and refusing to budge.

'What's up with you, Herman?' she said. 'You were like this yesterday. There's nothing to be scared of.'

She turned to the banana copse and then wasn't so sure.

She swallowed.

It no longer looked like a lovely painting. The grove had turned dark and eerie. Shadowy trees like beckoning giant fingers beckoned her in the dusky light. Insects shrilled a warning and a floral scent like an unwanted breath hung in the humid air.

She shivered. Her chest quivered.

She thought of turning around and going home, bananas or no bananas.

'You're being silly,' she said to herself.

Herman's odd behaviour was spooking her

'I'll just take the bananas and go,' she said. After all, she had brought a bag and a knife. She could just make out the pendulous bunches in the shadows.

As she stared into the grove, she had the sense of something or someone peering out at her. A hidden malevolence, waiting for her to step into it. A deathly darkness that would wrap its arms around her.

Perhaps *he* would be waiting there.

Her face went cold.

This time it wouldn't be his fists.

There would be a knife and he would use it to rip out her heart and slice her throat and a fountain of blood would spurt out.

'No more walks for you, baby,' the stranger that was her husband would say, his breath stinking of whiskey, as he swaggered from the banana grove. 'No more chocolates or perfume for you.'

The hairs rose on her arms.

Why did she think this?

'Stupid, stupid thought,' she whispered. 'He's at the office and he'll be back soon for dinner.'

Herman whined.

'There's nothing there, Herman. Just stupid shadows. Nothing to be afraid of. And I want those bananas and they're organic too. Not sure if the ones in the shops are truly organic, but these are.'

She pulled on the leash but Herman crouched stubbornly on the grass refusing to move.

'Well, I'll just have to tie you up then, you big coward.'

Herman eagerly followed her back up the slope to the nearest lamp post where she tied his leash.

As she turned to walk away, Herman barked at her. It sounded like a protest and a warning.

'What is it?' she said, frowning. 'Stop that barking.'

She pointed a finger at him. Herman whined and sat down, leaning his head mournfully on the lamp post.

'Good boy,' she said. 'Now be quiet. I'll only be a short while.'
Then she turned and walked towards the banana grove.

As she approached the beckoning shadows, once again, her face
went cold. The banana-leaf fronds swayed eagerly, too eagerly, in
the creeping darkness. Ever so keen to draw her in. The tightening
knots in her stomach told her not to go there, but to turn and flee.

And never, ever come back ever.

But another part of her, the rational part of her, of
online shopping, social media and cooking shows, told her
she was being dumb. That there was no reason to be scared.
That there were bunches of fruit waiting to be cut down. She
would give some to her neighbours, bake cakes and make deep
fried bananas.

She had come all this way and she would feel awfully foolish
going back empty-handed.

Pulling out the knife from the canvas bag, she stepped into
the shadows. Part of her felt as though she was being sucked into
a dark, dangerous grotto. But she ignored the feeling.

A leaf brushed against her cheek as she entered. There
was just enough light to see that the fruits were bigger than she
thought. When she was done cutting the first comb, she slid them
into her reusable shopping bag.

As she turned to the second bunch, she heard Herman
barking urgently. Then he began to whine as if terrified. As if he
was about to be ripped to shreds.

Her skin crawled. She felt a tingling on the back of her neck.

Someone in the heavy shadows behind her. She could feel it.

There was a bad smell too that made her want to hold her nose.

Then there came a low breathing noise. It seemed to come
from deep within the soil itself.

She didn't want to look. Didn't want to see what was there.
She thought of fleeing, out of the copse and into the street,
grabbing Herman and running home.

But, very slowly, her heart pounding, she turned.

Blinking, trying to make out what was before her eyes, she discerned a figure. Wearing a white smock, squatting, back propped against the wall. The face was hidden by long black hair that draped like curtains to the ground and merged with the mocking pools of blackness.

It whispered in a cold voice.

'I've been so waiting for you.'

* * *

Where the fuck is she?

He wandered up to the bedroom, paced aimlessly, fists clenched. Then he stepped into the bathroom and, in the mirror, saw a face he didn't recognize. He grunted, splashed water on his face, paced again in the bedroom, then sat at top of the stairs.

He waited, breath tight in his throat.

'Should have stayed at the bar,' he whispered. 'Instead of this.'

Alone in an empty house.

The woman needed to be taught a lesson. A damn good one. He wouldn't be kind like he was all those other times. Now he would really hurt her.

He was furiously messaging the bitch when he heard the front gate creaking open. Then the front door being unlocked.

She came in, shut the door and dismissively glanced up at him.

'I've been bloody waiting for you!' he growled and stood up. He made his way unsteadily down the stairs. Yeah, one drink too many. But so what?

She dropped the reusable shopping bag and its contents on the floor. The one that said 'This Bag Saves the World'.

As if one stupid bag was going to do that!

He hated these companies and their marketing bullshit. And right now he hated her ten times more.

'Where have you been, you stupid cunt? Where's Herman?'

His wife said nothing. Her face as blank as stone.

'Where the hell's our damn dog?'

Still she said nothing.

Bloody bitch.

He slapped her.

But to his surprise, she didn't recoil nor shriek in pain. She just stood staring expressionlessly like a statue.

He felt his blood boil.

'Come here!'

He grabbed her hair and dragged her to the living room.

Normally she would cry out, plead with him to stop in that pathetic whiney voice of hers as she stumbled along. But now she stayed silent and simply followed, keeping pace with him as if this was some kind of comical dance.

He released her hair, spun and, growling, punched her in the stomach. It was a forceful uppercut that usually dropped her to the floor like a rag doll.

His eyes widened. She simply stood there as if nothing had happened.

'What the hell's wrong with you!' he barked. 'You on drugs or something?'

But no, there was something else about her. Something so strange and horribly wrong.

'Answer me!' he snarled.

He slapped her again. A real hard one this time.

But her head stayed still as a rock. The eyes narrowing, yet somewhat amused. As if he was nothing but an ant to be squashed.

What the fuck?

His hand stung. Coldness tightened his guts.

On her stony face, the lips curled into a grin.

The hairs on his arms rose.

'Shit!'

He knew then, with an awful certainty, like a hook that jerked on his brain, that no, this wasn't his wife. The cold scrutiny in her eyes told him so.

The woman closed her eyes and slowly bent her head which allowed her hair to fall over her face. It glistened like velvety black curtains before a freak blood-soaked show.

Then something most odd started to happen. For the hair began to grow . . . longer and longer . . . all the way down to her hips. She grew taller too, which was impossible, but he saw it happening with his own eyes. And thinner she was too and, instead of the clothes she had on, her body was now covered in a loose dirty white garb that was stained with . . .

Blood!

Fresh blood . . .

He could smell it.

'Dear God,' his voice shivered.

He took a step back, heart pounding, not believing his eyes.

Slowly, the hair parted and the head rose to reveal the face.

What the hell!

He staggered back, tripped over the sofa and fell on it.

He sat there, amongst the cushions, insides squirming, watching madness unfold.

This was no woman but a creature, a loathsome thing with . . .

No eyes!

It was as if they had been dug out.

There were just black holes, chasms of madness, where the eyes should have been.

Its skin, wrinkled and slimy, was no colour of any human skin . . . of whatever race or creed.

This has to be a nightmare!

But no, it was too bloody real. It was happening right here and now.

The creature glided towards him. It stank of the sewer. Or putrefying meat in a rat-filled swampy darkness.

He clamped a hand over his mouth.

'So you've been waiting for me?' It said in a voice that loosened his bladder. 'Well, I've been waiting to meet you.'

It stroked his cheek with one cold, slimy finger.

This brought a shrieking in his head that almost splintered his mind.

It grinned, then it slapped him, the blow flinching his head sideways.

His scream fled up the stairs and echoed back down again.

'P-Please, please. D-Don't hurt me,' he managed to whisper. 'For the love of God.'

The demon threw its head up, its laughter high-pitched like a thousand tortured geckos screeching.

'There is no room for your god here,' it hissed, the dark hollowed-out eyes scorching into his. 'Nor is there any mercy. There is only your warm flesh, your precious blood, to fill my stomach.'

It smacked its mouth open to reveal long blackened teeth.

With a delighted-filled trill, it lunged, the fangs rising, then plunging into his neck.

As agony blazed through him, he saw himself beating his wife. Saw his sneering father advancing, removing his belt and striking him on the legs and back. But never, never on the face. Saw his mother whimpering in a corner . . .

Then these visions, that had come tumbling over each other, turned red like an engulfing pain. He felt his arms flailing, his legs uselessly kicking. His body shrieking till blackness swamped him.

When the demon was done feasting, it wiped its mouth, withdrew and turned away with a satisfied grin.

It left on the sofa a body soaked in blood, face etched in terror, stomach torn open, slippery spilled intestines half eaten.

As the demon glided down the driveway, it glanced at the woman's corpse it had earlier dumped beside a row of flowerpots. It looked like an animal's carcass, the flesh cold, its blood soaked into the dry soil.

The demon slipped out the front gate into darkness. Down the road, beneath electrical cables, past street lamps and houses, it was nothing but a cold watery shadow that drew all darkness to it. To those at home, whether watching a movie or eating dinner, they might have shuddered, momentarily feeling like some unspeakable evil was treading on their graves or pushing needles into their wax effigies.

Near the banana grove, it picked up the dog's carcass and flung it, leash and all, into the jungle which, for a long while, silenced the noisy insects and whooping monkeys.

Then it squatted in its lair, back against the wall and, in the darkness, licked its lips and waited.

Room 511

'That's bullshit!'

'I'm sorry, sir. I've checked again. I can't find your booking in our system.'

Tim Dobson glared at her. 'Look! Here it is on my phone. I booked it a month ago.'

Her smart grey uniform gleaming beneath the frosted lights, Kavitha glanced at the computer again and shook her head.

'I'm really sorry, sir. But there must be something wrong with the app. Your booking isn't here. I would give you a room but our hotel's full. There're a few big events happening this week. I can check with other hotels to find you a room.'

'Look, I've just arrived from Sydney. It's almost midnight Australian time and I'm bloody tired. I'm not going to another hotel. You have to honour my booking. So you better find me a room.'

'But, sir . . .'

'I'm not going to leave till you get me a room!'

Kavitha could see from the blistering lines on his face that the Australian meant it.

He glared at her across the marble countertop, face reddening. This was a luxury hotel and she didn't want him to cause a scene.

She knew of the one room that was available.

But should I risk it?

Her throat went dry.

Tim Dobson was muttering loudly to himself and several guests frowned their displeasure as they strolled by the reception area.

Kavitha bit her lip. She felt she had no choice.

'Please wait a moment, sir,' she said, forcing herself to smile at the difficult customer.

She tapped the keys, booked it into the computer and called housekeeping.

She lowered her voice. 'Sir, we do have a room. Can you please wait fifteen minutes for housekeeping to attend to it?'

He glared at her. 'There you go! So you do have a room after all. You really need to put your foot down to get things done around here.'

'If you could please take a seat in the lobby, sir. I'll come get you when the room is ready.'

He nodded grimly and strolled into the lobby.

Jeon, her Korean colleague, glanced at the computer screen, grasped her arm and whispered: 'You're letting him stay in *that* room?'

Kavitha bit her lip. 'There wasn't anything else I could do. He was going to cause a scene and disturb the other guests.'

Jeon nodded. 'Yeah, he was talking very loudly.'

'And he just wouldn't leave, Jeon. So I have to give him the room.'

'Well, maybe it's okay now. If there's a problem he'll just leave and go to another hotel.'

'Yep, he can always do that.'

Kavitha tried to grin despite a knot tightening in her stomach.

* * *

In every hotel worldwide there are some rooms that are never let out to guests. These are the problem rooms, where strange things occur with no natural explanation. Kavitha had been with this luxury hotel for several years and knew better than most that room 511 was off limits not because it was haunted in the ordinary sense of the word but because it was possessed by an evil spirit.

A trainee once mistakenly booked someone into it. The guest, an Eastern European woman in her sixties, fled in the middle of the night. She didn't even return to collect her luggage. Then just last year, the air conditioner in one room wasn't working and a guest from China was erroneously transferred to it.

The businessman was supposed to check out three days later but didn't. When housekeeping went to check on him, he was found naked on the bed, mouth open, tongue flopped out. But what scared her the most were the eyes, wide and filled with terror. The air conditioner was off and, in Singapore's hot humid climate, the terrible stench made her vomit, making it to the bathroom just in time.

So as not to alarm the guests, the body had to be removed at the dead of night. As she was on the late shift, Kavitha was instructed by the manager to supervise the operation. Covered in a white sheet, the fetid body was being taken out by two men from housekeeping. As they too were from China, they did the job with great empathy, sighing and muttering as they moved their country man's decomposing corpse.

Even though they all wore face masks, she still had to hold her nose. She stood just outside the bathroom to allow the two men space to push the trolley out of the room. As they did so, the trolley bumped against the transition strip between the room and the corridor.

Something cold and clammy jumped out and slid against her thigh.

Oh, my God!

A greyish hand dangled against her skin. One cold finger touched her thigh just below her skirt. For a second, she thought it would come to life and, like a scaly reptile, slide its way up her thigh in a slow chilling caress.

One of the housekeepers, eyes wide in fright, saw that the dead man's arm had fallen from the sheet. He hurriedly slotted the corpse's arm back on the trolley.

He gave her an apologetic look and pushed it out of the room.

As the body was wheeled down the carpeted corridor, Kavitha, still trembling, was about to close the door. As she did so, she heard something.

She cocked her head to listen. There it was again.

A whisper.

It echoed from deep within the room.

Boku wa . . .

Her hairs stood on end.

The voice was cold, grasping.

She slammed the door shut and hurried after the trolley, the whispering echoing like an evil snigger down the corridor.

She had studied Japanese on her tourism course, and she knew what it said.

I like pretty young girls.

* * *

Tim Dobson didn't want to kick up a fuss but sometimes you just bloody had to.

Assertive but not aggressive. The corporate world had taught him that. And it got results.

But perhaps he had overstepped. Well, he was tired.

'Great room, anyway,' he sighed, pulling off his shoes and tossing them beside the wardrobe.

The room was bigger than the one he had booked online.

He got a beer out of the minibar, sat on the armchair and drank half of it in a few gulps. Then he messaged his wife to say that the useless hotel managed to get him a room after all.

So everything's fine, he wrote.

But, after a long shower, as he gazed out at the city lights, it didn't seem so fine anymore. He thought he felt a whispering cold breath on his ear. He shivered and turned but there was no one there. Just the empty room staring back at him.

After sending out a couple of emails, he slipped into the large, soft bed, filled with an assortment of pillows.

He checked to see if his wife replied but she had not. It was late in Sydney.

He switched off the lights, clutched a pillow and forced himself to close his eyes.

Something about this room just didn't feel right. There was a cold, brooding presence. As if someone watched his every move.

'Just my imagination,' he whispered. 'Been a long day.'

He tossed and turned until sleep eventually found him.

But, a couple of hours later, a noise made his eyes spring open.

What was that sound?

He lay listening for a few moments, thinking that perhaps he had dreamt it.

It was cold and he was about to get up to adjust the air-conditioning when he heard it again.

Running water.

That was it and coming from the bathroom. Who the hell could be in his bathroom at this hour?

Housekeeping? No way.

Heart pounding, cold sweat on his palms, he slowly crept out of bed.

Then he switched on the lights and stepped into the bathroom.

But there was no one there. Just marble tiles staring questioningly back at him.

To his surprise though, the tap over the basin was gushing.

'What the hell?' he whispered, breathing hard, trying to work out how this could have happened.

He turned it off, looked quickly around, expecting an intruder to appear out of nowhere. But, to his relief, no one did.

Closing the door, he switched off the light and went to bed.

But he couldn't sleep. He lay listening, wondering how a tap could come on by itself, not wanting to think of ghosts.

Just as he was feeling drowsy, he heard something else.

The toilet being flushed!

He flicked the lights on and darted into the bathroom.

'What the hell!'

He blinked to make sure he wasn't seeing things.

The toilet paper roll lay on the floor and toilet paper streamed out in a convoluted mess.

'Christ Almighty!'

This was utter madness. What the hell had done this?

He cleared it up, thinking up all kinds of explanations. But he found none.

He didn't believe in ghosts, spirits and anything that wasn't bound to the realities of this world, and so he refused to consider the supernatural. He knew though that sleep wouldn't find him, and so he pulled out his laptop. There was always solace in work.

As dawn crept in through the curtains, Tim fell asleep.

* * *

After what had happened when they removed the corpse, Kavitha researched the hotel's history. Before it was a hotel, Japanese occupying forces had used it as a headquarters during the Second World War.

Locals and Allied POWs were regularly tortured here and so she was not surprised that the hotel was haunted. Over the years, local shamans of all varieties had been brought in to conduct spiritual cleansings and the building was eventually declared ghost free.

All except for room 511. Whatever was there refused to leave.

When Kavitha began her shift that night, she was relieved to see Tim Dobson. He stood at the lobby entrance with two men in suits.

She felt her shoulder being nudged. Jeon was grinning brightly at her.

'He looks fine after his night in the room. So don't look so worried.'

Kavitha shrugged. 'I'm not worried.'

Jeon frowned. 'Yes, you are. He's alive and well.'

'He looks pale and haggard though, don't you think?' Kavitha turned and stared at Tim Dobson who was now shaking hands with the two men.

Jeon lowered her voice. 'Well has he complained?'

'No, he hasn't.'

'So all's fine then.'

* * *

Tim Dobson went to bed early.

His head throbbed and he wished he had packed some paracetamol.

The strange events from the night before had exhausted him and so did the meetings today which didn't go so well. He had just one client to see tomorrow morning and would then catch the afternoon flight to Sydney.

'Hope I don't get woken again,' he whispered. 'It's just so damn strange. Don't think anyone back home will believe me if I told them about this.'

He imagined his wife coming up with various rational explanations. Suddenly he missed her and his three kids. He couldn't wait to get home.

Turning on the TV, he watched a bit of news. A celebrity wedding, elections, the stock market. Nothing so interesting.

Yawning, he switched off the bedside light.

A couple of hours later, the sound of the shower running woke him up.

* * *

The hotel was quiet which gave Kavitha lots of time to worry.

Outside the hotel's gleaming entrance, the concierge slowly paced up and down in his black uniform as if counting time.

She felt as if she was doing the same. Counting the hours until Mr Dobson checked out.

Why did she let him stay in that room?

Because she had no choice. That was the reason. He was kicking up a big fuss, disturbing the other guests.

But still, she wished she didn't let Mr Dobson stay in . . .

Something cold touched her thigh.

She gasped and jerked away.

The corpse's cold hand against her skin.

It had fallen from the bedsheet!

'No!' she almost screamed, then clamped a hand over her mouth in fright.

'What's wrong?'

She looked up at Jeon and blinked. She felt as though she'd just woken from a nightmare.

'J-Just my stupid imagination, Jeon. That thing from last year.'

Jeon frowned. 'What thing?'

Kavitha swallowed, then whispered. 'You know, the room. The haunted room.'

'Oh yes, the haunted room. So what about it?'

'I was thinking about that dead man from China and the voice I heard.'

Jeon bit her lip. 'Awful. Very awful.'

Kavitha nodded. 'What if Mr Dobson . . . what if he *dies* tonight. I'm going to call him, just to check he's okay.'

'But it's three in the morning!'

'Oh, I'll make some excuse, Jeon. I'll say we're checking for burst pipes.'

'Yeah, but stop worrying. I'm sure he's okay.'

Kavitha grimaced, picked up the phone and called room 511. Her face went pale.

'He's not answering. Jeon, can you please go check on him? You'd be doing me a huge favour.'

Jeon shook her head. 'Sorry, I can't. I'm scared too. You checked him in there. You should go.'

'Why don't we both go together, Jeon?'

'But we can't. Somebody needs to be here at reception.'

Kavitha shivered. 'I suppose I have no choice then.'

Jeon crossed her arms. 'You'll be fine. Don't worry.'

But Kavitha did worry.

She left the reception and headed for the lifts.

* * *

Kavitha paused, her finger over the doorbell.

Why didn't Mr Dobson answer the phone?

Is there something really wrong?

Perhaps it just wasn't working. That was why he didn't answer it.

But deep down she knew that wasn't the reason. Something had happened to him. Just like that man from China.

I have to help him!

She swallowed and pressed the doorbell.

She heard the familiar chime but no one answered.

She pressed it again.

Still no response.

Something awful's happened. I just know it.

She slipped out the master keycard, unlocked the door and pushed it open.

She was met by a brooding darkness.

'Hello,' she softly called. 'Mr Dobson? It's Kavitha from reception.'

No answer.

The hairs rose on the back of her neck. She felt something watching her, hiding in the gloomy shadows.

Then came a sound from the bathroom.

Running water.

Then the sound of someone shuffling inside.

'Mr Dobson?'

She heard a voice, low and echoey. It sounded like: *come in, my dear.*

She didn't want to, but she had to make sure he was okay. Then she could get back to work with her mind at peace. So she stepped into the room and switched the entry light on.

Except it didn't work.

Suddenly, the door slammed shut behind her.

Kavita shrieked.

Heart pounding, she could hardly breathe.

Within the darkness, she glimpsed a shadow, a huge black cloud, blacker than black, sliding, creeping, slipping against the wall.

Then the sudden smell. A dead man smell. Like that corpse touching her thigh, cold against her skin, just below her skirt. Almost alive as it reached for the panties.

The same awful smell. But much worse.

Her heart was racing.

Have to get out of here!

She spun around.

Grabbed the door knob. But the door refused to budge.

Then hollow footsteps right behind her.

And deep breathing, cold like ice against her neck.

A voice whispered: *Boku wa . . .*

I like pretty young girls.

'Nooooo!' she screamed as she felt arms grabbing her.

She spun around to see a mass of pulsing blackness engulfing her body.

Cold, so cold . . . was the evil embrace.

For a second, she glimpsed a smooth-faced, grinning man in a uniform wearing a peaked cap and round glasses. On a table, neatly arranged, were metal torture instruments. The man picked one up and deliriously laughed. A drop of blood on his spectacle lens. Then came shrieks, cries, groans as victims were whipped, fingers cut off or smashed in, bodies hanging like dead goats from the wall.

The deep breathing was louder than before, echoing like a monstrosity in her head.

She was being dragged.

No! Please no!

She tried to fight back, to get away, but the shadow-mass, bound her limbs and was too strong, too merciless.

She was flung across the bed.

'I'm not having this, damn you!' she cried.

She tried to get up but was pushed down.

She gasped as her head hit the mattress.

It grabbed her breast, squeezed it painfully. A tongue slid down her neck, wetting it up to her ear lobe. It bit her neck. A long love bite.

'Get off me, you bastard!' she yelled.

She tried kicking and punching the entity, this mass of evil blackness, but her limbs felt like dead-weights.

A cold, cold hand, a cadaver's hand, slipped up her thigh and jerked her panties.

'Noooo!'

This thing wanted to rape her.

Then kill me? Like the man from China?

She was sure of it.

'Please, please . . . don't!'

Suddenly, a burst of light struck her eyes.

The door had been flung open.

Jeon stood looking at her, light from the corridor spilled on her face. 'What the hell are you doing there on the bed?'

Kavitha opened her mouth but could only gasp.

Jeon grabbed both of Kavitha's arms. 'What happened here?'

Kavitha, body trembling from cold and fear, tried to sit up.

'Wait, let me help you. Your body's shaking all over. Are you okay?'

'I . . . I'm fine,' Kavita whispered.

But she didn't feel fine. She'd just been attacked by some dark entity. An evil spirit.

'You're going to be okay,' Jeon said. 'I've got you,'

Kavitha nodded.

Her colleague had come in the nick of time. She had likely saved her life. Saved her from being raped and killed.

Jeon glanced around. 'Is . . . is the guest here?'

Kavitha shook her head.

'We better leave before he comes back.'

Jeon held Kavitha around her shoulders and led her out of the room.

* * *

Kavitha couldn't stop shivering and gasping as she told Jeon what happened.

It felt as though the dark entity was just behind her. She turned around a couple of times but there was nothing there.

When they reached the safety of the lobby with its marble pillars, leather armchairs and indoor palms, Kavitha glanced into the casual dining restaurant that served the daily buffet breakfast.

It was empty but for a figure, head slumped on a table.

She tugged Jeon's arm. 'That's . . . that's Mr Dobson.'

The waiter told them that Tim Dobson had been there since after midnight. He had ordered a snack, did some work on his laptop before falling, snoring loudly at the table.

'Now we know why he wasn't in the room,' Jeon said as they made their way back to the reception desk. 'He was in the restaurant the whole time.'

Kavitha nodded. 'Maybe something had scared him.'

'Yeah, maybe. Maybe that's what happened.'

'I shouldn't have gone to check on him then. But I was just so worried.'

Jeon touched Kavitha's shoulder. 'Anyway, he's leaving tomorrow. So no need to worry anymore. You look so pale. Are you sure you're okay?'

'Yes . . . I'm fine. Just a bit shaken.'

'Our shift ends soon. You can go home and rest.'

Kavitha tried to smile. 'Yes, Jeon. I need that. I really need that.'

* * *

When Kavitha got home to her flat, the first thing she did was to check for marks on her neck. There was a small bruise but nothing serious.

'A love bite from a ghost?' Kavitha whispered to her pale reflection in the mirror and shivered.

Was it perhaps an insect bite? No bloody way. Insects don't give their victims a wet lick on the neck or fling them on the bed or try to pull down her panties.

There was no other explanation.

Suddenly she felt exhausted. She could hardly move her limbs. She normally had a hearty breakfast before her sleep but now she had no appetite.

Must be all the excitement.

But it wasn't excitement. It was trauma.

'You're lucky to be alive,' she whispered at her reflection in the bathroom mirror. 'I should get Jeon some flowers or chocolates or something. It's not every day that someone saves your life.'

She managed a smile, then slipped off her clothes.

In the shower, she shampooed and soaped herself vigorously, desperately wanting the warm water to wash off the memory of the thing attacking her.

After she dried off and changed into her sleeping T-shirt, she drew the curtains and, as usual, secured it with clothes pegs to keep the sunlight out.

'Wish we were back on day shifts,' she said tiredly as she pulled the blanket over her.

Night shifts messed up the body clock and she could never get a proper sleep. And after what happened this morning, she didn't think she could sleep at all.

But she did.

Except that an hour later, her eyes flicked open.

A cold, awful feeling gnawed at the pit of her stomach.

Why . . . why did I wake up?

She had heard something.

There it was again, a noise in the bathroom.

Running water.

She swallowed.

No, it couldn't be. Not here. Not now.

Her heart was beating fast.

Then the sound of the toilet being flushed.

'Shit! Oh, shit!'

She gripped the blanket tightly as if it would offer some protection. But that was a foolish notion.

No, this can't be happening! Please!

Cold sweat dripped down her forehead.

Very slowly, the toilet door creaked open.

Followed by hollow footsteps.

Her bed creaked.

I like pretty young girls.

The Elevator Game

'Sure you want to do this?' Sara asked, her streak of pink hair falling across one side of her face. She was twenty-three, a couple of years older than me.

'Yes,' I said, yawning. 'That's why we're here, aren't we?'

Sara nodded. 'I'm getting sleepy. The coffee isn't helping much.'

She wore a white tank top which exposed a hummingbird tattoo on one pale shoulder.

I glanced at my phone.

2.10 a.m.

The twenty-four-hour coffee house was deserted.

'You're gonna start the shoot soon?' she asked.

She was a makeup artist who hated wearing make-up. She didn't need it. She was no typical beauty but her petite frame, intelligent eyes and smile made her irresistible. We'd been together for a few months and had a loving relationship, so unlike the disaster of my previous one.

'Let's go soon,' I said. 'There shouldn't be anyone using the lifts. But I'll post something first.'

I snapped a few selfies, chose the best ones, cropped and filtered them, then uploaded the photos. Everyone did social media. Tell the world what you're doing and privacy can go to hell.

Gonna start the shoot guys, I thumbed. *Don't wanna get stuck in the other world. Wish me luck!*

Of course, I didn't believe in the superstitious nonsense. But I believed in viewers for that was all that mattered.

My head thrummed with excitement. My new video was going to send my viewer-numbers skyrocketing. I'd been promoting it for the last few days. Before, during and after the shoot were essential.

It was going to be fun for I was going to do . . .

The Elevator Game!

Some YouTubers had several million views playing it. I wanted to beat them all.

I slipped a comb out of my back pocket and ran it quickly through my hair. My hair didn't need it but the routine made me feel good. 'Okay, I'm gonna start.'

Picking up my phone, I began the shoot.

'It's just after two in the morning,' I whispered to the lens. 'Yeah, I'm pretty nervous. I'm playing the elevator game or lift game, as we say here. The game originated in Japan or Korea and I'm gonna do it now.

'You play the game by taking the lift to various floors. It's a set sequence which must be followed. I've written it on my wrist, so that I won't forget.'

The game was a bit complicated so I had to explain in carefully. I slowly moved the phone over my wrist to see what I'd written there:

G - 3 - 1 - 5 - 1 - 9 - 4 - G

I flicked the phone back to my face, trying to look deathly serious. I was getting quite good at acting.

I'd already summarized the game on social media but people didn't read, preferring photos instead. They were basically dumb and lazy which was great for, while they watched adverts, I made money.

'It's time to find out if it works. So let's go!'

Continuing the shoot, I swaggered through the hotel lobby as if I was a celebrity influencer rather than a first year Computer Science undergraduate. Sara followed cautiously in the distance as she wasn't supposed to be in this part of the video.

'I've chosen this hotel,' I said, 'because it's old and they don't use keycards to get to the various floors. Just makes it easier.'

And then I whispered, eyes wide. 'And some people think it's haunted!' This wasn't true, but it sounded good. Showmanship, which included a generous layer of bullshit, was essential.

The hotel receptionist behind the counter glanced at me. I nodded at him and he nodded back.

'He must think I'm a guest here,' I said. 'So no problem.'

I continued walking, chatting and keeping the phone at a high angle, as I approached the lift lobby.

Then, glancing back to check that Sara was still following me, I stopped in my tracks.

A figure lurked at one side of the hotel entrance.

It slid malevolently behind Sara, as if shadowing her from a distance. I couldn't make out the face nor clothes for that part of the hotel was badly lit. But something about the way it moved, the way the head hung like something dead sent a shiver up my spine . . .

I swallowed.

Then the figure was gone. As if it had merged with the concrete pillars.

What the hell . . . who was that?

I switched off the video.

Sara ambled into the lift lobby.

'How's it going so far?' she asked.

I just stared at her and blinked.

'Everything okay, honey? Your face is so pale.'

'Oh, eh, I'm cool.'

I didn't mention the strange figure stalking her, the one that I felt was now watching me. My mind was going nuts. Perhaps I wasn't getting enough sleep.

'Hold on,' I said.

I went around the corner and peeked into the hotel lobby. It was deserted except for the lone receptionist. But why did

I feel there was someone else. Someone watching. I felt foolish. My mind had to be playing tricks.

'What are you doing?' Sara asked.

'Just checking.'

Perhaps it was my head that needed to be checked. This was crazy.

For a moment, I thought of abandoning the shoot . . . but that was crazy and, before I could stop myself, pressed the lift button.

I tried to grin. 'Okay, you better head up now. So wait for me at the fourth floor, okay?'

Sara nodded. 'Okay, see you soon. Don't get scared when I get into the lift later.'

I managed a low chuckle. 'I won't even look at you. But I'll pretend to be petrified.'

There were only two lifts and the left one chimed.

Sara slipped in and gave me a wave as the doors slid shut.

Pulling out my phone, I began to video myself again.

'I'm at the lift lobby and, so guys, this is where the action starts. Anyway, the game is played like this. I'll ride the lift to those floors I wrote on my wrist in sequence. And the scary thing is that on the fourth floor a woman may enter the lift. Now, she's from that other world. That's shit scary and I'm not sure if I want to do this.'

Suddenly, the thought of the shadow stalking Sara made me realize that I wasn't fully bullshitting. Maybe this wasn't a good idea. Maybe the elevator game isn't something to mess about with. But I wanted to make this video and it would be a huge success.

So don't be a scaredy-cat.

I thought a voice whispered. I spun around, except for a painting of a row of colourful shophouses on the wall, the lift lobby was empty

This was ridiculous. I was spooking myself.

Feeling like an idiot, I returned to the phone.

'Anyway, the last floor I need to go to is back here on the ground floor, but if the the game works, unknown forces will make the lift mysteriously rise up to the 9th floor instead! And, guys, that floor belongs to a different world!'

I doubted anyone had ever made it to that different world without being high on drugs. I almost laughed, but managed to stop myself.

'To finish the game, I need to go to all those different floors again but in the reverse order. Anyway, wish me luck!'

I pressed the button, waited, heard the chime and stepped in.

The interior was older in style with tinted mirrored walls and, separated by a wooden rail, a dark timber panelling ran down the lower part. A framed poster on one wall promoted their weekend afternoon tea of cakes and savouries served on a multi-tiered platter and definitely social-media friendly. It would be a nice place to take Sara to celebrate my YouTube success.

I pulled out a second video cam from my pocket, switched it on and placed it on the floor in one corner. I continued videoing myself on my phone. A two-camera set up worked well.

I jabbed a floor button. 'Now, let's ride to the third floor.'

The lift hummed its way up and the door slid open. I did a quick shoot of the lift lobby and part of a corridor that led to the hotel rooms, all covered in a dark grey carpet. The doors slid shut.

'Now for the first floor,' I said, raising my eyebrows, grinning nervously, which may have been real, and stabbed the lift button.

The lift hummed its way down and again the doors slid open and shut.

I did the same for the fifth floor, followed by the first and ninth floor. On each floor, I did a quick shoot of the lift lobby and corridor which all had the same dark grey carpet and light grey patterned wallpaper.

'It's chillier now,' I whispered for effect, even though nothing had changed. 'The air seems a lot thicker.'

I wondered if Sara was getting impatient waiting for me to arrive on her floor. My viewers, millions hopefully, would be shocked to see a young woman stepping into the lift. Her face would be turned away so that even my friends who knew Sara wouldn't recognize her.

Smart people would, of course, know it was a set up. But it didn't matter. Anyone with any sense knew reality TV was fake yet people still couldn't get enough of it.

When Sara did step into the lift, I was going to quietly gasp and perhaps even stagger back, to show how bewildered I was. But I had to be careful not to overdo it.

I jabbed the lift button. 'Okay guys, now for the fourth floor. This is the one where some young woman might step in. It feels very chilly now, not sure why. I'm really nervous.'

I wrapped one arm around my chest, clutched my shoulder and pretended to shiver as if I was in a meat freezer.

I continued to video the lift's digital display as it hummed its way down.

9 - 8 -7 - 6 - 5 - 4

Ding.

The lift door slid open.

But there was no Sara.

Someone else stood there.

* * *

A tall woman wearing big sunglasses, a black cap and a grey jacket stepped in. She wore bright red lipstick and there was a hint of perfume.

She glanced away from me as she entered as if she didn't want me to see her face. Then she stood in one corner of the lift, her back facing me, the toes of her sports shoes almost touching my second video cam. Her head pressed into the corner, right up against the lift walls' two mirrors.

Shit!

Hairs rose on the back of my neck.

What is she doing? Who the hell is she?

Could it be?

No, this was just a game.

Where was Sara? And who was this woman?

I took a deep breath. Perhaps she was from that other world. No, I didn't want to think of that possibility.

Fingers trembling, I carried on the shoot. I had no damn choice.

Breathing hard, I stared speechless into my phone, my face cold.

I jabbed the button for the ground floor, hoping the lift would not later shoot back up to the ninth floor as might happen in the game. Because, this other-world could right now be standing in the lift with her back to me.

My phone chimed. I almost dropped it because my hands were shaking.

A video call from Sara.

With trembling fingers, I managed to press the 'accept' button.

'H-Honey,' she whispered.

From the expression on her face, I knew something was terribly wrong. Her face was contorted in pain. Then I realized she was sprawled on the floor.

'Sara,' I gasped. 'What the hell . . .'

'I . . . I'm hurt . . .'

She turned the phone towards her body. I glimpsed the hummingbird tattoo on her shoulder, then I saw something dark on her white tank top which I thought was spilled coffee.

Sara groaned. 'Someone . . . stabbed me.'

Blood! It was blood!

'Who? What the hell!'

This was crazy. I couldn't believe that this was happening.

'An . . . ambulance. Please . . .'

I nodded desperately. I had to save her. She could be dying!

'Yes, yes, I'll call them now. Where are you?'

'In the fire escape.'

'Hang on, hang on.'

Her eyes were blinking, lips quivering.

'I-I love you, honey.'

I placed a finger on the phone's screen. 'I love you so much too.'

Then my phone flew out of my hand, hit the mirrored wall and clattered on the floor.

The lift went *ding*. The doors slid open, then shut.

The woman had knocked the phone out of my hand. Her lipsticked mouth curled bitterly and behind the big sunglasses I felt her fury.

I gasped. I didn't care if she was from this world or not.

'Why the hell did you do that?'

'Don't you know?'

Her voice was icy cold. And . . . and . . . familiar too.

'No, no I bloody don't!'

'I followed your girlfriend up to the fourth floor and there I stuck my knife into her belly. Three times. Oh, she squealed like a pig!'

My mouth fell open.

No, no, that's bullshit!

Before I could angrily hit her, she stepped back and grinned.

'Then I dragged your lousy girlfriend into the fire escape stairwell. She's not so lovely now, is she? All bleeding and life seeping out of her?'

That face.

Beneath the cap and sunglasses, I . . . I knew that face!

'H-Hanna,' I whispered.

'Glad you finally recognized me, sweet darling.'

She slid a large knife from her jacket.

Before, I could do anything, she stepped forward and drove it into my belly.

I grunted and staggered back, hitting the back of my head on the lift wall.

I collapsed to my knees, moaning, my stomach ablaze.

Clutching my stomach, I fell to the floor, struggling for breath.

The ceiling lamps blazed into my eyes, shifting in and out of focus. One part of me couldn't believe this was happening. That this was a nightmare, and I would soon wake up safe in bed, Sara cuddling me beneath the blanket. But another part of me, knew that it was happening here, right here, right now. One minute I was making a video and next I was on the lift floor in agony, warm blood flowing over my fingers.

Hanna jabbed a lift button.

She grinned. 'To the ninth floor we'll go. Up and up and up!'

'W-Why?' I groaned.

'It's the elevator game, isn't it?' she said. 'It's so much fun. I saw it on your social media. That's how I knew you'd be here tonight.'

'W-Why did you . . . stab me, Hanna?' I whispered, clutching my belly.

'Don't you know, sweet darling?'

Spittle dripped down her chin.

The lift chimed and the doors slid open.

Grabbing my shoulders and muttering to herself, about how heavy I was, she dragged me over the grey carpet and into the lift lobby.

She pulled off her cap and sunglasses and flicked them to one side. Her hair, together with its abundant curls, fell about her shoulders. With her false eyelashes and grey contact lenses, the bitch almost looked attractive. 'You should never have left me. We were so good together.'

I blinked at her. I wanted to scream: *No, we weren't!*

But held my tongue.

Since the day I fled from her apartment, she had been hounding me, trying to get me back. Sending me tonnes of messages and emails, some pleading, some abusive.

'You're so foolish making this video,' she spat. 'Playing some dumb game made by some bored Japanese fourteen-year-old. But people like scary, don't they?'

I swallowed, not knowing what to say, my stomach burning.

Her eyes were wide with excitement, as if she was thoroughly enjoying herself.

'So it was the perfect opportunity. But when I saw you in the lift, I didn't know if I could do it. So I just stood in the corner. Then your girlfriend called and you were both so lovey dovey. And I couldn't stand that! So here I am, all for you!'

'W-Why?' I spluttered. 'Tell me why?'

But I already knew the answer.

I came to know that she was mentally unstable in our few months together when she cut up my T-shirt with a pair of scissors because she was jealous. Now I knew she was totally bloody fucking mad.

She grinned fiendishly and flashed the blood-stained knife before my eyes. 'To kill you, of course. If I can't have you then nobody will.'

'No, no, don't. P-Please, don't.'

'You wanted to see the other world. Well, you're going to see it now!'

She did a quick little dance, wielding the knife, hopping from side to side like a demented clown.

'D-Don't do it, Hanna. Please!'

She lunged at me, her eyes brimming with mad ecstasy.

'Welcome to the other world.'

She licked her lips, lips that I had once so passionately kissed, and in a single swift motion, she slashed my throat. An unbelievable pain screamed through me. I grabbed at the open wound as warm blood gurgled down my neck.

She smirked. 'That's you taken care of, my sweet darling. Now I'll need to go find myself another boyfriend.'

A feverish chill fell over me as a spasm went through me.

I was dying and there was nothing I could do about it. A million viewers couldn't save me. And Sara . . . my poor Sara, I couldn't save her either.

The last thing I saw before darkness descended was Hanna winking at me, satisfaction in her mad lipsticked grin, before she tossed her hair back and pressed the lift button.

* * *

Sara succumbed to her wounds in the fire escape stairwell five floors below, her phone tightly clutched in one hand. She had bled to death, waiting for an ambulance that never arrived.

As for me, I died in the hotel's lift lobby on the ninth floor. They had to replace the blood-soaked carpet.

My phone and second video cam were found in the lift. Some lucky person uploaded my elevator game videos on YouTube. After the sensational murders it went viral with millions of hits. But I was not there to claim neither fame nor riches.

Such is life. Or death.

The lift or elevator game is still played around the world. It's done for fun, for a bit of thrill. Mostly nothing happens but whether a few manage to open that door to that other world, we can't be sure.

As for me, I find myself lingering on at the hotel, mostly wandering aimlessly down the grey-carpeted corridors, standing in a shadowed corner of the lift lobbies or riding up and down to the various floors.

Sometimes you can hear me sighing as you press a lift button. Or the doors may slide open at certain floors only to find nobody there. Or you may feel a sudden chill as you ride through the various floors for I am right beside you, hoping, just hoping you'll play the elevator game with me.

Cathedraphobia

I'm Global Sales Director for a successful global company. So a big deal you may think. After all, I frequently travel.

Business class. Five-star hotels. So pretty cool.

I'm lounging at a swanky hotel restaurant with an old friend who is understandably envious.

'So you get to see the world, huh? All expenses paid!'

I grin, nod and sip coffee.

'What's your favourite city then?'

'Hmmm . . . maybe Tokyo, Seoul. London and Paris, of course. Perhaps San Francisco, Berlin, Singapore. Sydney too.'

'Oh, you lucky bastard. I wish I could travel like you.'

'Well, I work bloody hard too.'

'Of course you do. And very well paid I'm sure!'

Again, I grin, nod and sip coffee.

Global Sales Directors reap a hefty salary. Some like me travel extensively and collect heaps of frequent flyer points. Most useful for exotic island holidays.

We exit the hotel and shake hands. While he hurries off to hail a taxi, I step into the hotel hired car and head for the airport, cabin-luggage beside me.

Frequent-travellers travel light.

As I watch buildings slide past, glass and steel, hard-edged, soaring, no-compromises, I shift in my seat. A tightness in my throat.

In the glare of sunlight, I glimpse my own reflection.

I spoke not the truth, even to my old friend.

I hate travelling.

Long-haul flights don't bother me much. I even enjoy hours of solitude, wrapping my mind around problems, tapping and clicking the laptop, perhaps even watching a movie.

Undisturbed. No phone calls.

Nor is it the endless meetings or time away from my wife and young son which led to the divorce.

Is it the unending series of hotel rooms?

Five-star and luxurious they maybe. But every room holds an unknown history. Even mysteries.

What restless heads have rested on its fluffy pillows? Whose bared feet shuffled on its thick carpets? Whose bottoms perched on the cold plastic toilet seats? What secrets have soaked its walls?

Although the hotel room with its past and secrets do at times concern me, it is something else.

You see, I suffer from a phobia.

There are many phobias around, of course.

The more common ones are: Claustrophobia, fear of confined spaces; Acrophobia, fear of heights; Aerophobia fear of flying; Agoraphobia, fear of open spaces; Zoophobia, fear of animals; Cynophobia, fear of dogs; Escalaphobia fear of escalators.

Mine is somewhat odd . . . a fear of *chairs*.

Cathedraphobia.

So don't you laugh.

Pretty damn ridiculous, right? Big shot Global Sales Director that I am?

Sofas are perfectly fine with me. Nor do I have a chair problem in my day-to-day life. I can sit in a meeting room with twenty empty chairs with no concerns other than a slight sweat on my palms. What's more, chairs with people in them miraculously make the mental anguish disappear and I run my meetings effectively and with composure, without the slightest hint of discomfort.

For me, the big problem is a chair in a *bedroom*, which includes any hotel room.

There's invariably a hotel writing desk with its smart, designer-like reading lamp and a room-service menu on it and beside the desk will be that *chair*. A most problematic piece of furniture. The traditional looking ones bother me most, especially wing chairs.

Once my wife bought one just to spite me. She placed it in our bedroom and when I returned from my business trip the wing chair was in the corner by the window staring me in the face. The ugly thing was light grey with a single row of buttons on the backrest. I felt leeches crawling on my skin and had to stop myself from fleeing.

'Why the hell did you buy that?' I gasped.

She liked wearing men's pyjamas and she stood there in her favourite khaki one, hands on her hip, staring at me, a cold determination in her face.

'I want a divorce,' she said.

I'd been resisting for months. Hoping somehow that we could patch our lives up. That going to that marriage counsellor could actually improve things. But now I saw it was no use. Her message was more than clear. There was no going back.

'You can have it then!' I spat. 'Now get that damn chair out of here!'

'No, I won't. You can sleep on the sofa. You and I are done!'

And so I did.

I moved out a couple of days later to a studio flat in the city. I told the bemused landlady that I didn't need the two dining chairs and she promptly removed them.

So I hate travelling.

Alone in a hotel room, my eyes can't help but be drawn to the chair, to its grotesque shape, that vacant seat, usually cushioned, demanding that someone or something fill it.

Ever since my wife brought that wing chair into the sanctity of our bedroom, when I stare at any hotel-room chair, I discern faint shadows within its seat and the backrest darkens, smothered by a mass of grey, turning to black.

I swallow. Close my eyes. But it's no use.

For in my mind, I already see it.

The blackness coagulating into a thin horrid figure reclining there, leering at me even as I turn to face it. I now know the reason for my fears: it is because I imagine *something* sitting there.

* * *

Here I am in one of my favourite cities and enjoying the taxi ride through its clean traffic-jammed free streets. I'm glad that I'll be staying in a recently renovated highly recommended luxury-brand hotel overlooking a river that courses through this modern city. We business-folk can't be expected to travel like backpackers, can we?

Stepping out of the hired car, I glance up appreciatively at the hotel's white walls, the stuccos, porticos and columns of the imposing early twentieth century colonial building and the contemporary glass-steel tower abutting it.

The red-uniformed concierge flourishes the door open, and I step into the lobby's air-conditioned coolness, my shoes clicking on the marble floor, feeling that this is where I belong. This cavernous space is furnished with Edwardian-styled sofas, ottomans and coffee tables, softened by a plethora of lush indoor palms grouped around soaring white pillars.

'You're in the heritage wing,' says the pretty young woman at the check-in counter as she hands me a key card. 'We hope you like your room, sir,'

'I'm sure I will.'

I grin for I know I mean it. If she'd join me though, I'm sure that I'd like it even more. Call me sexist but I reckon that, deep down, all men are.

I grin as I wheel my cabin luggage to the lift lobby. The antique-styled lift, with a poster of folks having fun at a cocktail club on level two, whooshes me away. I wheel down the carpeted corridor, swipe my card and enter.

The hotel room is well-decorated in the same Edwardian manner as in the lobby. Fleur-de-lis patterned crimson curtains flow elegantly down to the thick-pile carpet. A large TV screen sits above a dark-timbered dado. A gold-painted framed print of a fox-hunting scene on the wall, a bucolic landscape in the background.

Very nice indeed. I'm sure that I'm going to be extremely comfortable here.

I drop my jacket carelessly on a bed piled with pillows and bright cushions and wander up to the large, mullioned window.

The view's good too. Not spectacular but better than a brick wall.

Tourists and locals are wandering in small groups along a muddy-coloured river. The tropical late-afternoon sunshine turns the pavement bright orange. A Chinese man wearing a straw hat sells ice-cream from a metal cart beneath a grey umbrella and, from the long queue, business seems good.

I turn from the window and feel as though I've been punched in the stomach.

A wing chair.

I can't believe that I didn't see it before.

Upholstered in a black-and-white pattern, it's huddled beside a walnut cabinet where sits a Nespresso machine. Against the dado adjacent to one side of the bed, the four-legged fiend stares back at me.

Cold sweat drips from my forehead and I feel my heart pounding.

I've never had a wing chair in my hotel room. *Not ever.* The sight of the upholstered creature before my watering eyes makes me nauseous. The rows of buttons on the backrest remind me of the scaly skin of a sea serpent.

I grab my wallet, key card and flee the room.

Breathing hard, I keep my eyes on my shoes as they hurry me down the corridor, into the lift, through the lobby and out into the sunshine.

I gulp mouthfuls of air. The youthful Malay concierge frowns in his red uniform, then smiles at me. I ignore him and head towards the river.

Not knowing what to do, I join the queue for ice-cream, then, melting purchase in hand, aimlessly meander down the river-track, eyeing fellow walkers and boats plying the muddy-coloured waters against a backdrop of soaring glass-concrete buildings.

Cathedraphobia. That's my curse.

Wing chairs, the worse.

Professional help hasn't been of much use. It's a fear I face on my own.

I think of changing hotel rooms or moving to a different hotel. It's an option but this phobia has to stay my secret. It's been my oldest friend, my greatest enemy. And perhaps it's high time I confront my fears.

I stroll along the river trying not to think about it and instead study my fellow-strollers, the boats plying the river and the modern buildings on the other side.

Having arrived from a noisy crowded city draped in winter grey, the warm sun on my back manages to lift my spirits and I push the wing chair to the back of my mind. I even manage to enjoy myself.

My thoughts soon focus on unfinished business, to emails demanding replies, calls to be returned, agendas and issues to prepare for tomorrow's meetings.

Work calls and I have to return to the hotel room.

* * *

I don't want to look at the four-legged fiend.

Instead, I march around the bed, slip out my laptop and hunch over the writing desk facing the window, keeping the offending object behind me and safely out of sight.

I will attend to it later, I tell myself. Exactly how I'm going to do that though, I'm not quite sure. But right now work calls.

I continue working until the sky turns purple and the darkness that follows is impressively lit by the cityscape. After making phone calls and replying to numerous emails and no longer able to concentrate, I order room service: steak, salad and fries.

Plus a bottle of red.

I'm going to need it.

Not being a big drinker, my head is woozy after downing half the bottle with dinner, all the while eyes on the cityscape, ignoring the thing staring at my back like some jealous lover or hungry demon. I can't be bothered to call room service to clear the tray and instead place it, used plates and all on the walnut cabinet beside the Nespresso machine. Housekeeping can remove it in the morning.

I do all this without giving the wing chair a single glance.

It's only after a long shower, then slipping into my pyjamas my wife once bought me for Christmas, that I decide it's time to confront the thing.

I stand before it now. My face tight. My throat dry.

Heart beating hard.

My solution to every chair in the hotel room has been the same. I have always, even though I've tried to stop myself and chiding myself that I need to confront my fears, carried the offending object to the bathroom, propping it in the shower or bath, its back against the tiled wall.

I now try to do the same with the wing chair. I slide the heavy item across the carpet, grunting and cursing, but then, as I push and shove, I realize that it won't fit through the door, its armrests being too bulky.

'Shit,' I whisper. 'Stupid fucking chair.'

I leave it beside the bathroom door. It can rot there for all I care.

'How the heck am I going to sleep with you over there, staring at me?'

But I have to confront my fears. This is that opportunity.

No more putting chairs in the hotel bathroom for me. Maybe, if I'm tough on myself, I can do it. Just have to find the courage to overcome the phobia.

Sleepy or not, I sit on the bed, eyes on the fiend and, trying to be brave and, not realizing it, slowly polish off the rest of the wine. But my throat is dry just watching it. My heart thumping raggedly like a murder of crows in my chest.

Although somewhat tipsy or perhaps because of it, I consider fleeing down to the cocktail club on level two. I could return blind drunk and collapse on the bed, not giving a rat's arse about the chair.

I decide it's a dumb idea for, with meetings lined up tomorrow, I need a good night's sleep. Coward that I am, I switch on the bathroom lamp, leave the curtains wide open to allow light to spill into the room and slip beneath the quilt.

Head on the pillow, I realize I can see that damn chair every time I open my eyes. And, if I can see it, then . . . *it can see me too!*

'No, no, no I have to move you.'

So I drag the thing back to where it was before, beside the walnut cabinet where sits the room service tray and Nespresso machine which I'm sure I'm going to need tomorrow morning. Three cups just to feel normal again.

All this drama over a stupid chair!

Perhaps there are some pills I can take for this. But they'd need to be so strong that they'd more likely send me into a bloody coma.

With the fiendish furniture back against the wall on my left, I decide I can now sleep on my right side facing the window and the glittering cityscape, my back to chair.

So should I open my eyes during the night, I'll see the window, not the chair. With that thought, I feel I can breathe again.

It takes me awhile but eventually sleep claims me.

But I wake up, head feeling warm. It's still night.

Through the window, the office blocks brightly glimmer and my first thought is about fools that work at this time of night. My second thought, makes my heart lurch.

The wing chair.

I feel its horrid presence coldly stroking my back.

Other than the humming air-conditioner, there's another sound.

I swear I can hear it *breathing.*

A crazy notion, of course, but slowly, very slowly, I turn in bed.

At first I only see its bulky shadow, four stout legs on the carpet, protruding wings, armrests, backrests big and breathing like a large animal.

But that's ridiculous. Wing chairs are inanimate, and they don't bloody breathe.

My eyes adjust to the darkness and slowly I see it for what it is. Just a chair. A piece of furniture. Nothing to be afraid of.

Silent. Still. No breathing sounds.

But my throat is dry.

A chill slips up my neck, for within the chair shadows are darkening. Thickening into a single mass. A heaviness that is drawing all blackness, all foulness towards it.

No!

There is that breathing sound again. Louder now.

And the shadow is solidifying.

I blink, not believing what I see.

But it is there.

A figure.

Just like the one I'd been seeing in my head.

A thin silhouette lazily lounging there as if it had been there all this while. A chill grips my chest. My heart is racing, as my eyes are transfixed on the skeletal figure, its face partially blocked by one upholstered wing.

Slowly, like a coffin opening, it leans forward, and a pale head falls into view. Light from the window slides upon putrefying skin. Long greasy hair creeps to its waist. Garbed in a dirty-white dress, no more than rags, the bathroom's dim glow slants upon one bony hand, one finger tapping against the armrest, eager for what is to come.

Then, as if it knows I'm watching, this woman-thing very slowly, neck creaking, swivels its loathsome head towards me.

The eyes, white sightless eyes are staring into mine. And I, unable to breathe, am staring back. I can't look away for my chest is heavy and, paralyzed by mounting fear, my limbs, my head refuses to move.

It smells of a thousand dead things rotting.

Slowly, the figure gets up from the chair, bones creaking as knees and elbows move in slow exaggerated kabuki-like way, a murderous puppet in a death dance. It treads over to the bed, foul breath rasping, slimy long fingernails reaching, one eyeball half-rotting slips out and, held by a sliver of flesh, dangles in the half-light. A long pale tongue licks its lipless mouth, and its evil grin turns my stomach liquid.

I try to scream but its sharp teeth is already in my throat and my own sticky blood soaks the pillow. As I feel myself falling into a chasm filled with voices shrieking and claw-like hands grabbing at me, all turns pitch black.

* * *

I open my eyes, blinking.

The glare of sunlight streams through the window.

A view of the cityscape. Breath spills from my throat.

It . . . it was just a nightmare.

The wing chair . . . it must have brought this on.

Drove my brain haywire. Sent my imagination into over-drive.

That bottle of red would have helped it along too.

I frown.

Didn't I also drink something else, a couple of cocktails perhaps?

A cold shiver clambers up my chest.

I realize that I'm not in bed but . . . but . . .

Sitting on the wing chair!

My heart is racing. My mind spinning.

What the hell am I doing in it?

My arms rest upon its sticky armrests, my shoulders on the buttoned backrests. An upholstered wing pressed against my temple. I am held in its awful slimy grip.

Gasping, I leap out of the wing chair as if the thing is on fire. I scurry over to the window, breathing hard and stare out at the river, shivering, trying to understand what has happened.

I'm not prone to sleep walking. It's something I've never done.

So why did I get out of bed in the middle of the night to sit on that four-legged fiend? Did I want my enemy to be my friend? Is this how my subconscious wants me to confront my fears?

I have no answers. Instead I massage my throbbing forehead.

Damn hang over.

The bottle of red. Cocktails too?

The ice-cream man is busy beside his metal cart, a small queue in front of it. A couple in bright running outfits is jogging along the river. Above the cityscape, the sky is dotted with clouds.

I must have slept in for it must be mid-morning. A beautiful one.

My nostrils though twitch for there is an odour. An unpleasant one. I turn to see a pillow on the floor.

'No,' I whisper. 'Can't be . . .'

Blood drains from my face.

On the bed is a sprawled woman. Naked with one arm dangling over the edge. At one time, she must have been beautiful but now her face is bleached and dead eyes are transfixed on the ceiling.

Her throat is black for it has been sliced open and the white bedsheet is soaked red.

I stand there gaping, trembling.

Memory floods my brain.

No, I didn't go straight to bed last night.

Of course not. Instead, I pulled on my clothes and staggered to the cocktail club on level two. After a couple of drinks, I brought this young woman, at an agreed fee, back to the room.

Once we'd had sex, I slipped out of bed and used the knife from the room-service tray. Steak, salad and fries. Slice of woman too. First in her belly. Then her throat. The blood-slicked blade now gleams upon the pillow, beside her tangled hair as if asking for more.

My heart is no longer pounding as I stare at my own naked body.

There's blood stains on my hands, my forearms. Even on my stomach.

Killing is such messy business.

I wipe them off with the bedsheet and slip into my pyjamas.

My mind is calm, cold like a mountain stream.

I glance at the Nespresso machine coffee. I hope they have Colombian.

As I wander over to the walnut cabinet to examine the coffee capsules, the doorbell chimes.

'Housekeeping,' a muffled voice calls.

Picking up the knife from the pillow and slipping it against my back, I approach the door.

I glimpse the wing chair staring at me. I see its black-and-white upholstery, its stout legs and bulky back, wings and armrests and am no longer afraid.

We're friends now, it says. *We can do things together.*

'Of course,' I whisper back. 'They can all be afraid of me.'

I open the door a crack.

There's a petite Chinese woman in a pale blue uniform and a white apron in the corridor.

'Can I make up your room, sir?' she says.

'Of course,' I reply with a winning grin. 'It's a bit of a mess. So please, come in.'

Baby Dream

I stepped out of the car.

Insect voices filled the air. Thick jungle all around.

Then Taylor Swift blasted through nature's chorus as Sofie came out, phone blaring.

'Is everything okay?' Sofie asked as she eyed me from the grassy verge in the shade beneath a clump of trees. She wore a new orange silk blouse and it made her look much younger than thirty-four.

'Just a puncture,' I said as I inspected the back tyre.

I opened the boot, pulled out the jack and the spare. Getting out the manual from the glove compartment, I followed the instructions to replace it. Sofie watched, asked the occasional question but mostly hummed as her phone played her favourite songs.

Several cars drove past. An elderly man on a motorbike stopped to ask if we needed any help. I thanked him and said that we were fine.

'Okay then,' he said, glancing into the jungle. 'But take care around here.'

I frowned. 'Why?'

'Just be careful.'

His eyes didn't meet mine and he looked almost sorrowful as he rode off.

'Maybe he wanted us to tip him for helping,' Sofie said.

'Yeah,' I said. 'Maybe.'

By the time I'd finished, my armpits were soaked and I yearned for a cold drink. I'd been driving for two hours from Sofie's mother house in a small town surrounded by palm oil plantations. She had celebrated her sixtieth birthday dinner last night, where there were cold drinks aplenty. I needed one right now.

'Okay,' I said, wiping sweat from my brow. 'It's done.'

Sofie turned off the music and insect shrills once again filled the air. Birds loudly called timeless melodies. She frowned and glanced up at the surrounding trees.

'Hey, do you hear that?' she asked as I put away the jack and punctured tyre back in the boot.

I turned to her. 'Hear what?'

She gestured towards the jungle. 'That crying sound.'

I listened and heard nothing at first.

Then there it was. A child wailing.

Sofie's mouth fell open. 'It's a baby!'

I frowned. 'No way.'

She grabbed my arm. 'It is, it is! Just listen, will you.'

I stared into the trees. 'Hmmm, it does sound like a baby. But there's no way there's a baby out there in the jungle. Must be some kind of bird.'

'That's not a bird!'

'Well it could be a baby monkey. Come on, let's go. It's hot out here.'

'I tell you it's a baby!'

'Look, what's a baby doing out in the jungle? It just can't be. Has to be an animal of some kind. Let's go.'

'No, I'm sure it's a baby. Someone must have abandoned it up there in the jungle. Or maybe the baby's there with its mother and the mother's died or fainted or something.'

Her face spoke of a desperation that I hadn't seen in our six years of marriage. We'd been trying so hard to have a child.

We'd done the IVF thing, spent so much money on it, but we were still childless. Having a baby, she had said would complete her life. It would be a dream come true.

I frowned. 'But it's up there in the jungle. How are we going to get there anyway? It just can't be a baby.'

But Sofie wasn't listening to me for she was already walking up the road, searching for a possible track into the jungle. I shook my head, locked the car and followed her.

This was bloody ridiculous.

'Come on, Sofie,' I called out. 'Let's go.'

She turned to me, that strange desperation still on her face. 'I can still hear the baby, can't you. It must be hungry or in pain or something.'

I could still hear it. It was fainter now but, I had to admit, that it still sounded like a baby. But it just couldn't be.

No way. Babies and jungles just didn't go together in our modern world. Sofie was being stubborn. Once she had something in her head, she didn't know how to let it go. I had to somehow talk her out of her crazy conclusions.

I sighed and turned towards the car.

Then I saw something that made me swallow.

Across the road was a narrow track leading up into the jungle. Sofie must have missed it in her excitement.

But should I tell her?

I didn't want to go tracking into the jungle. It would be sweaty, muddy and full of mosquitoes. Maybe leeches too. And where would the track lead to anyway? We could easily get lost. Perhaps it led nowhere but a dead end.

I didn't want to tell Sofie about the track but then I knew I would feel terribly guilty if I didn't. And what if there really was a baby and we could have saved it?

'It's over there,' I called and pointed before I could dwell on it further. 'See?'

At first Sofie didn't notice it, then her eyes widened. 'Yes, it's there. A path into the jungle!'

'Do you really want to go into the jungle?' I asked. 'It might be dangerous and . . .'

But I couldn't finish my sentence as she was already heading for it, striding with determination in her face.

Hurrying after her, I could still hear the faint baby's wail. If it really was a baby.

I took Sofie's hand, helped her up onto the track and we began to follow it into the jungle. This was really crazy but I knew that nothing was going to stop Sofie.

Insect sounds became a cacophony and the crying fell away. Twigs, leaves and branches pushed against our faces. Rocks and thick roots like sleeping snakes tried to trip us as a mass of ants meandered in long trails over the dirt and dead leaves. Sweat dripped off my brow as we wended our way up the steep slope.

I hated feeling hot, hated the notion that something might bite me. Mosquitoes, bees, ants, snakes, leeches. I hated them all. I wished I was back in the comforts of my car with the air-con at full blast.

I hoped the track would come to a dead end soon and we'd have to turn back. Sofie would be disappointed and most likely by the time we got to the car, the bird, baby or whatever it was, would have stopped its crying and we could head back home to our lives.

But there was no dead end.

Instead the narrow track widened. Sofie glanced at me, her face brightening. Still there was nothing to see here but a mass of trees, undergrowth, vines, ferns and insects both flying and crawling.

Thankfully, nothing had bitten me yet. No mosquitoes, bees, nor leeches.

Then I heard it, very faintly at first.

The crying.

Sofie clutched my arm. 'You hear it?'

'Yes,' I whispered. 'It must be up ahead.'

'I told you,' she said, triumph in her eyes. 'We need to get to it quickly. Who knows how long the baby's been out here. Maybe mosquitoes have bitten it all over.'

I was going to tell her that maybe it was just a bird or a baby monkey, but decided not to. She would just argue. But maybe, just maybe, she was right . . .

We continued to follow the track, which got even wider. It made several turns as the cries got louder. Then the path straightened and levelled out.

The cries suddenly stopped as if it, if it was a baby, didn't want to be found. Or perhaps it was just saving its energy now because it knew we had arrived.

Up ahead was a clearing dappled in sunlight. A large moss-covered rock stood in the middle of it. The boulder was unusually shaped, like a misshapen elephant I decided, and as we got closer, I wondered if it had once been carved. Perhaps it had become a shrine for the clearing looked swept recently.

I was about to mention this to Sofie when she rushed forward and knelt before something on the ground.

I hurried over and at her feet was a bundle swaddled in a white cloth. Sofie gently pushed open the cloth and there before us . . .

Was a baby!

I gasped.

Sofie's mouth fell wide open.

The baby's eyes were closed. It was asleep.

For a long moment, we both just stared.

'I told you,' Sofie finally whispered. 'It's a baby. A beautiful baby!'

'Yes, yes,' I whispered back. 'You were right. You were absolutely right.'

We grinned at each other and a tear trickled down Sofie's cheek. I touched her face and, with my finger, gently wiped it away. Our eyes slid back to the bundle of joy. The baby seemed so peaceful and glowed as if it was so happy to be found. Occasionally, its lips moved as if it was mumbling in a blissful dream.

'What shall we do with it?' I asked, frowning.

Sofie glared at me. 'Take the baby home, of course. We're not going to leave the baby out here!'

I glanced around. 'But maybe it belongs to someone. I don't know what the hell it's doing out here in the jungle?'

'Can't you guess? It's been abandoned and left to die. Can you see its mother anywhere around? No, it's been left here by some unwed mother, a teenager probably, because she didn't know what to do with it.'

'But why in the jungle?'

'Could be any number of reasons. Maybe she gave birth here in the jungle because she didn't want anyone to know. It's very sad.'

Then she grinned, triumph in her eyes. 'But for us, we now have a baby! *A dream baby!*'

Very tenderly, as if she knew exactly what she was doing, she picked up the bundle and cradled the baby in her arms. I helped her up as she held the baby against her bosom in a most loving gesture.

'At last,' she whispered and grinned at me.

She was bursting with joy.

I hopelessly knew that there was nothing I could do to stop her keeping the baby. She wasn't going to let the baby go.

I nodded reluctantly and managed to smile back.

Then the three of us proceeded back down the track.

I turned to look back several times to see if there was someone following us. Perhaps a mother chasing after us, screaming that we were stealing her child.

When we got to the car, Sofie sat at the back with the baby. Maybe she needed more room back there but part of me wondered if she thought the baby was more hers than mine. I pushed the foolish notion away.

Sofie was beaming with joy and I was incredibly happy for her. I was still worried about the mother though. What if she came looking for her child?

We got to the city after five and hit the long queue of cars at the toll booth only to be met by an endless line of vehicles crawling their way back home.

I glanced back several times to see Sofie cuddling the baby and either smiling radiantly or humming a tune. I was worried that the baby would wake crying and hungry. But it didn't.

On our way home, we stopped at a pharmacy and I bought powdered milk, feeding bottles, disposable nappies and other essentials. I think this was when it dawned on me.

The baby was ours!

We arrived home soon after. The house had three bedrooms, one master bedroom and two others for children, kids that I thought we might never have but right here, in Sofie's arms, was our first child.

Our first child.

It was a strange thought that came out of nowhere.

Our first child.

I was now determined to keep the baby. The mother, if she was still around and wanted her child back, would never find us. The baby was ours.

Sofie gently placed the bundle down on our bed upstairs. As if reading my mind, she whispered: 'Our baby. This is our baby and she's come home.'

'She?' I asked. 'How do you know she's a girl.'

'Of course, she is. I just know. A mother knows these things.'

I grinned. Sofie had suddenly become a mother. And I was . . .

A father!

What a strange and wonderful thought.

The next few days seemed to pass by like a dream.

And so we named our baby Dream.

Sofie and I both took turns carrying and feeding our child. Dream was so good and hardly cried and slept most of the night through. The baby cot I ordered arrived via express delivery and was easy to set up. I remembered those few days as the happiest in my life.

But at the back of my mind, I still had one thought.

What if the mother comes looking for her?

But how could she? She didn't know where her baby was.

Sofie wanted Dream to sleep in our bedroom for the first few months and so we placed her cot against one wall beside the dressing table. Dream spent a lot of time on our bed though so that Sofie could lay beside her and watch her softly sleeping.

Sofie was bursting with happiness. At last we had our baby. Now I understood what the term, bundle of joy really meant.

Our family and friends were thrilled for us and Dream received many gifts and toys.

Dream proved to be such a delight in our lives and it was no surprise that she became a precocious and intelligent toddler. As for Sofie and I, we didn't have any more children but we didn't mind. We had our wonderful Dream.

The years passed and our beautiful daughter won prizes in English and Maths and was captain of the soccer and badminton teams. We were so proud. She was always smiling, happy and obedient.

Still more years passed and how quickly they did. But I didn't mind. Really.

As I began to bald and Sofie added on several kilos and we both needed reading glasses, Dream breezed through high school and would soon be graduating with a Chemical Engineering Master's degree from a top US university.

Now in our fifties, we had downsized to a large apartment. We were looking forward to a holiday in the US after attending Dream's graduation ceremony.

'What more could we as parents ask?' I said to Sofie one evening after dinner as we sat on the balcony, cold drinks in our hands, admiring the city lights and thinking how blessed we were.

'Nothing,' said Sofie. 'Nothing at all.'

We grinned at each other and laughed.

* * *

That's what might have happened if events had unfolded as we wanted.

It was a yearning we may have had when we were trying so hard for a child. But, as so many of us have learnt and will discover things don't often go the way we planned.

Something we ignore at our peril.

So when Sofie picked up that bundle of joy that morning in the jungle clearing and holding the abandoned baby against her bosom, I didn't expect anything odd or extraordinary, certainly nothing to be concerned about.

So I didn't expect the white cloth to ripple without the slightest hint of a breeze. It half fell off the baby's body as if being tugged by invisible hands, revealing a small back that looked so strange. Well, quite ugly, in fact, which was most disturbing.

Then there was that stench of urine and a smell that . . .

Reminded me of dead things.

And, when I looked closer, I got a better look of the baby's back.

It was a mottled grey and hairy!

Without warning, two grey arms, long and spider-like, slithered out of the white bundle and grabbed Sofie by the shoulder while the other slid around her waist.

She shuddered and her face went pale. 'W-What's going on?'

'I d-don't know,' I muttered as I staggered back, not believing my eyes.

'Get it off me!' she cried. 'This, this . . . *thing's* no baby!'

The creature that we had mistaken for something sweet and helpless clambered up past Sofie's bosom and, with a sound like lips smacking, buried its big mouth into her pale neck.

I stood petrified.

What the hell was it doing to her?

And what the fuck were those long spindly grey arms?

The back of its skull was a sickly grey and it quivered against Sofie's neck as if in ecstasy. Several ugly bumps like tumours protruded down its spine and these throbbed in a slow rhythmic way beneath the speckled sunlight.

This thing was making a slurping, smacking noise as the tumours continued horribly throbbing.

The rest of the cloth now fell to the ground to reveal long, spindly insect-like legs and large claw-like feet.

Shaking my head in disbelief, I stumbled back until my shoulder struck the elephant-like boulder. I stood there, the coward that I was, unmoving, hands trembling, sweat dripping down my nose, until I heard Sofie shrieking as if hell had suddenly opened up.

Blood sprayed from her neck, two warm drops struck my cheek. One fell on the dirt just short of my colourful Nikes and a demented part of me was relieved my expensive shoes were spared.

Sofie staggered, body swaying.

She howled as if she was being boiled in oil.

The creature was still buried in her neck, its spider-like arms still desperately clutching her with an intensity beyond any craving.

My dear wife sagged to her knees and, with a final wretched cry, collapsed to the dusty ground.

I stared at her, at the creature that still clung to her, not believing my eyes. Not believing this was happening. It was a nightmare. Yes . . . had to be.

For in the real world, babies don't attack people, do they?

But there was that slurping, smacking noise which sounded louder, more desperate, awfully and hideously real . . . telling me that this was happening right here, right now.

This was no nightmare.

'Noooo,' I moaned and I stumbled over to my wife.

'Sofie!' I cried, falling on my knees several feet from her, for I was too petrified of the sucking creature at her neck.

Her eyes were open, terrified eyes that stared.

Black ants, disrupted by her fall, scurried over dead leaves, tree roots and her hands, fingers and wedding band.

'Sofie, get up!' I cried.

But she didn't answer.

Her body was stiff, her eyes were unmoving, fixed upwards at the blur of sky.

Still there was that loud, sucking sound, echoing horrifically in my head.

'Noooo!' I cried, for I knew. Knew that . . .

She was dead!

'Damn you!' I screamed.

I grabbed the creature's cold, slimy body and tried to pull it off her neck. But it was fastened too tightly, clutching onto Sofie in a sickening embrace.

Then, heart pounding in fury, I grabbed a fallen branch and smashed the back of its grey skull with it.

For a second it didn't move.

Then the head spun around and it snarled.

It was high-pitched cry, filled with hate that made my stomach squirm.

The burning-red eyes brimmed with anger.

It stank of blood and urine.

Its open mouth, dripping with Sofie's blood, revealed a row of sharp fangs.

I backed away, my legs shaky, my heart pounding, for I realized that this creature was a . . .

Vampire!

The creature leapt, arms letting go of Sofie and clawing at me as the long, spindly grey legs pushed off the ground and the vampire soared through the air.

By sheer luck its fangs failed to find my neck for as I stumbled back, I tripped over a tree root and fell.

Instead of grabbing me, the creature's long arms flailed at empty air and it crashed into the boulder. There was a thud and a high-pitched muffled shriek.

Laying on the ground, dirt against my face, I saw that the thing lay sprawled motionless. Its grey head was turned toward me, eyes closed, long arms and legs splayed out, the naked body, baby-like in size, bulging with horrid-looking tumours.

I crawled over to Sofie, not believing this was happening. For how could it, in this modern digital world which left no room for spirits nor demons?

Her eyes were wide-open in a terrified expression, staring up at the trees that screamed at the sky. Blood soaked through her orange silk blouse which had been partly ripped, revealing a black bra.

I touched her cheek and shook her small shoulder but it was a useless, hopeless gesture for she was dead. Her throat all ripped out, black and bloody. Bits of flesh like wriggling red worms clung to her skin.

'No,' I groaned. 'No, no, no . . .'

My tears dripped to the dirt as I knelt beside her, my body trembling with grief, wondering how hell had suddenly arrived on earth.

Then I heard an animal-like scratching.

Slowly, with dread clutching my heart, I glanced back and saw long grey fingers curling and uncurling in the soil. The vampire's eyes flickered, then they opened and red eyes burnt into mine.

Shit!

Slowly, I stood up, eyes not leaving the creature.

'Leave me alone!' I cried.

Like a small animal, the vampire got to its knees, wiped the dirt off its limbs and snarled, spitting out bits of blood and saliva.

Its high-pitch cry echoed like a chainsaw through helpless trees.

Heart pounding, I turned and fled.

Twigs and leaves viciously struck my face as I ran down the track, breathing hard.

The creature was after me. Had to be. It wanted to rip my throat out.

Sofie was dead. There was nothing I could do.

I had to save myself.

I stumbled down the winding track like a babbling idiot, moaning in utter fear, not caring about the scraping branches, expecting the vampire to pounce on my back at any time, its vicious fangs biting into my exposed neck.

I glanced back once, and, to my relief, saw no sign of it. Just the winding track and trees and snatches of angry sky above. Still I leapt over rocks and tree roots, hurtling down the track.

Suddenly, sunlight struck my eyes as I tumbled onto the grassy verge beside the road.

My car!

There it was. Not more than fifty meters away.

I jumped up and sprinted towards it, almost laughing with delight to be out of the jungle and to feel the sun on my face.

I scrambled into the car. Slammed the door shut.

I had made it!

I felt like jumping for joy. I was going to get out of here. I was going escape from the creature.

Then for a horrible second I thought that the car might not start. I had seen it in too many movies.

My face went cold.

'Please!' I cried as I jabbed the ignition button and the car . . .

It started!

'Yes!' I cried with both relief and triumph.

That creature could go to bloody hell, where it belonged. It wasn't going to get me. I was safe in here.

I slammed the car into gear, pressed the accelerator and it shot smoothly out onto the road. The road that would take me safely home, away from this horrific nightmare.

'Yes!' I yelled. 'Fuck you, vampire! Fuck you!'

Just to make sure, I turned for a final glance at the jungle.

At the start of that track that led us to madness, the shimmer of green and the tumult of trees.

No sign of it.

'Yes, I'm going to be fine!'

I'd escaped from the blood-sucking creature. It had probably retreated back up the track into the jungle where it belonged. It could ambush someone else but not me. Not today, not ever.

All I had to do now was . . .

A shadow, like a giant bat, shot through the air. It came crashing down on the windshield.

'No!' I cried, losing control of the car.

The car spun and veered off the road.

It crashed headlong into a ditch

I must have blacked out . . .

But only for a moment.

Moaning, I slowly unclosed my eyes.

Leaves and twigs pressed against the shattered windshield. The foliage rustled in a gentle breeze. Scattered sunlight and shadows fell over the car's crumpled bonnet.

'I'm . . . I'm here,' I whispered. 'I'm still alive.'

I sighed in relief. I rubbed a hand on the back of my neck. It was sore but I didn't care. My arm was numb too but that didn't matter either.

I was damn lucky, I had survived the crash

'I'm going to be okay. Good thing I'd put on the seat belt.'

I didn't even realize I'd done it. It was an automatic action hardwired into my brain. If I hadn't, I would have been thrown out through the windshield and I would be dead or paralyzed for life.

But then, as a bead of sweat trickled down my forehead, I realized those were the better alternatives . . . yes, much better . . . for now the greenery rustled and revealed a grey shadow squatting on the car's bonnet.

Red eyes stared into mine.

It was scrutinizing me, the way a diner stares at a sumptuous meal.

Lips curled into a wide grin as it crawled towards the shattered windshield on its long spider-like limbs, its animal-like breath spilling from its half-open mouth.

'No!' I moaned. 'Get away!'

This couldn't be happening. I had escaped the thing. But now it was here. Coming for me.

I tried to unfasten the seat belt but it didn't work.

'Please! Please! Fucking open!'

I pressed the latch desperately over and over with trembling, shaking fingers but it refused to unlock. The seat belt still held me fast as if conspiring with the vampire now squatting before me.

It cocked its head and one long finger tapped the broken glass, eyes bright, mouth drooling.

Tap, tap, tap.

It grinned a wicked grin.

'Please,' I whispered, my heart pounding, my breath ragged. 'Please don't . . .'

But it was, of course, useless. It would feast on me, like it did poor Sofie.

The creature's tongue flicked out and it began to drool as if it understood.

Its mouth slowly opened to reveal long white fangs.

So this was it, this was my end . . . my bloody end.

In a single high-pitch yelp, filled with greedy delight, it smashed the windshield and lunged into the car.

I shrieked.

Blood like rain splattered the windows.

And all turned red.

The Garden

The old woman's eyelids flick open.

Through the broken roof, dappled sunlight creeps like a pack of yellow geckos upon the weather-blackened walls. A chirp echoes from the big tree but this can be no bird for no such creature lingers in these haunted gardens.

'Just my imagination,' she whispers.

She knows the chirping is in her head. And it says things to her.

Traffic whooshes on the main road beside the house as always, increasing from year to year, even as the mess and tangle in the garden grows wilder, darker as more and more foliage join the tumult and the rusty chain-linked fence sags itself into near collapse.

She heaves her body from the metal-framed bed with its thin, stained, damp mattress that smells of mouldy dead things.

'Or maybe me,' she whispers.

For is she not already decaying on the inside, right within her squirming worm-like guts? Squatting, pushing her wiry white hair from her crinkled face, she wonders if she has forgotten something, a something that hides on the edge of her thoughts. But what does she care for memories? They just plague her days and gouge out her eyes at night. And in the morning some other monster screws them back into her skull. Yes, that must be so.

So that she can behold these miserable surroundings!

She slips on rubber slippers and shuffles across a tiled floor covered in broken ceramics, glass and things once useful, even treasured, but now long discarded.

Abandoned . . . just like her.

And treasured? By whom? Yes, she did treasure them once but she was then some other woman, one long dead and gone. Shaking her head as if to toss the memory away, she steps into the wreck of a kitchen.

One wall has collapsed revealing a dark forest garden in a sun-drenched neighbourhood. She crosses the broken-tiled floor, steps over the collapsed wall and squats amidst rubble and a mass of dead leaves. She sighs as her urine is greedily absorbed by the dry soil.

Picking up a plastic doll with one eye missing, she shakes her head and tosses it upon plastic rubbish bags. Mounds of them have grown into barrows as months passed into years and years into more miserable years. How long has she lived in this squaller she doesn't know. It was once a delightful house with a pretty garden and a rambutan tree up front, but those memories have long deserted her. She has allowed her garden to run wild into something dark, brooding and oppressive.

A black furry thing darts away, tail flicking as it burrows beneath several bags of rubbish, some with their contents spilling out like rotting intestines. If she had the energy, she would hunt the rat out, club it to death and roast it for breakfast. But no, all she has is mouldy bread hanging in its plastic packaging on a picture hook on her cracked bedroom wall.

An elderly couple used to visit every week or so. She didn't know who they were, perhaps Christian or Buddhist do-gooders. They used to leave a plastic supermarket bag hanging from the front gate. The last one had tinned sardines, a packet of biscuits, a loaf of bread, some rice and several over-ripe bananas. But that was weeks ago. Since then she has been hungry.

Very hungry.

* * *

The estate agent's Proton SUV is parked close to the beach, around the corner from the no entry street sign and the house where the passion fruit vines drape over the street-side wall.

Afternoon sun reflects off the condominium towers, slants upon her pale round face and warms her short hair. She is thankful for the occasional sea breeze that slips in between the houses to momentarily draw away the heat of the day.

She eyes each bungalow and thumbs the occasional note on her phone.

The ones that are recently renovated are splendidly designed and built big while others are like old beggars on their knees and some are abandoned, gardens over-grown, windows broken, wall paint black and peeling. These brick corpses crumble and rot in the sun.

She feels like a corpse too. Or soon to become one.

When her husband arrived home last night, she wanted to ask him why he was late and not answering messages, but instead simply asked: 'How was your day?'

He didn't answer but stared at her as if she was a bundle of dirty laundry before going silently upstairs, his shoulders hunched as if he was sinking with each slow and dreadful step. Guilt, that was what it was. Had to be.

In his eyes, she feels that she is already dead. A corpse rotting.

Unlike the renovated houses, how can she come to life again? These decrepit time-ravaged bungalows can easily be sold if the price is right, if the owners weren't so greedy. New owners will pour money into them and contractors will bring them back to life.

But, for her, what is there . . . but separation, then divorce? Their marriage is a house, crumbling to dust before her eyes. At least they have no children.

She takes a deep breath.

Must focus on work.

Is she over-dressed in a beige skirt and a matching jacket over a white blouse? She needs to look professional . . . especially today, when she's door-knocking. Guerrilla-marketing in this online world. But no one likes to be disturbed at home.

She has managed to talk to two owners but they said they didn't want to sell. Not right now anyway.

She turns a corner and is stopped in her tracks.

The house is more than abandoned. It is an utter ruin.

Its sorrow, its utter misery, leaches into her heart, turning it to dark despair. Some walls have fallen and the holes in the roof are mouths crying in pain. Engulfing the ruin is a garden cramped with vines and trees turning it dark and brooding like a haunted forest.

She squints into the shifting shadows and gasps.

Squatting like a spectre beside a collapsed wall is an old woman.

* * *

The old woman looks up, eyelids blinking. Then a gleam settles in her eyes.

At last it is the couple bringing her food.

Oh, it's been far, far too long!

But no . . . it's a plump woman . . . standing at the front gate in heeled shoes and beige jacket, peering in through the rusty grilles.

Dressed like that, this person, whoever she is, must work in an office. She must be selling something.

The estate agent tries to make out what the old woman is doing squatting there unmoving. She raises a hand in a greeting and pushes open the front gate. The gate creaks loudly and gets stuck on the pavers and only opens ajar.

She squeezes through the opening, and picks her way through the driveway covered in dead leaves and thorny weeds.

Nodding and smiling at the old woman, she enters the darkness of the garden-forest, pushes her way through the tall grasses, a desolate figure beneath black branches, leaves hanging blood-like. She stops some distance away, her progress blocked by mounds of rubbish bags.

'Good morning,' she calls. 'Are you the owner? I can help you sell your house.'

The old lady scratches her wiry hair and stares, suddenly irritated by the intrusion.

'I've sold many houses in this neighbourhood,' the agent continues. 'I can get you a very good price.'

The old woman coughs, bites her lip. Her stomach is cramped. 'The other side,' she rasps.

'What other side? Where?'

'Front door. Other side.'

The agent nods, turns and makes her way back. When she gets to the weed-infested driveway, she looks around uncertainly then turns towards the front side of the house.

The old woman rises when she hears her front door creaking open. She trudges through the mess of a kitchen, her makeshift bedroom, the burnt-out living room, the black walls and caved-in roof, to see the agent standing motionless at the entrance, face pale and uncertain.

'Welcome,' calls the old woman, though she doesn't mean it.

Or does she?

Often she can't tell what goes on in her head.

The agent jerks back, the mouth dropping open, eyes blinking as if she'd suddenly woken from a dream. She has the sudden notion that coming here was a bad idea.

Eyes now stare wide at each other. Two women, the tracks of their lives intersecting at this ruined corridor at this singular point in time.

The old woman creeps forward, eyes never leaving the agent's face. As she draws herself along the damp wall, she is not surprised if the agent turns and flees, for the agent's expression has turned into one of disgust, even fear.

But it is her job, her work, her survival, her very being that makes the agent stay.

'M-My buyers . . . they will like your place,' she stammers, not knowing what else to say. 'They prefer to demolish and build rather than renovate. Your house is perfect.'

A twitching finger rises to her nostrils as if the house smells bad.

The old woman knows that can't be, it is this failing body of hers. When was the last time she washed herself? The water was turned off years ago.

She grins reassuringly and gestures for the agent to follow.

'Come look,' she rasps. Her stomach is tight, squirming.

The agent is unsure if she should follow as the old woman shuffles down the corridor. But she has come this far and doesn't fortune favour the brave? Did she first hear that expression from some action movie long forgotten? At the cinema with her husband, holding hands in the dark? Or was it a motivational video for property consultants?

She grimaces and tails the old woman into the living room and is glad to step from shadows into the brightness falling in from a gaping hole in the roof. One of the walls is badly charred. A fire from long ago? How can anyone live in such squalor? Does anyone ever visit her? Why isn't she in a nursing home?

The old woman nods to herself when she hears the agents swishing footsteps following. She leads her from living room to bedroom, a vague humming in her head.

'I just need you to sign an authorization form. If you agree, of course.'

'Yes, yes,' croaks the old woman.

She steps over an empty plastic Sprite bottle and enters the kitchen.

'I can get you a very good price,' she says to the back of the old woman's head. 'It's a very good time to sell. I'll just need your signature.'

Once she has that she'll quickly leave. Back into the sunshine and fresh air. And then she'll just . . .

Did the old woman just chuckle?

The old woman turns and an eagerness in her eyes sends a shiver down the agent's spine, like cold blood dribbling.

The old woman gestures beyond the collapsed wall. 'Birds no longer come here. Only rats. And now you . . .'

The agent turns to the fallen wall, the garden-forest . . . its dense foliage quivering in a semi-darkness carpeted by strewn rubbish bags and layers of dead leaves.

Something chirps and she glances up at the higher branches.

So she hears it too.

The old woman slides one gnarled hand along the kitchen bench and finds the chopper.

As she feels its weight, she remembers the time she used to slaughter chickens in the wet market. That was when she was still a teenager, well before she met the lanky man who courted her even though she was so poor. Eventually, despite his family's objections, they got married.

But what has happened to him? He left and never came back, not even once. But no matter . . .

She slips in from behind like a slippery lizard. With one hand, she slices the exposed throat, cutting easily through the flesh. The agent makes no sound. There's just a gurgling as she sinks to her knees and blood gushes from the wound.

The old woman grins.

She will be eating today.

* * *

Rain.

Falling hard. Hasn't rained for weeks.

But now it is. Yes, it really is!

The old woman, belly full, steps out into the garden, making a path through the mounds of rubbish bags. Wiping grease from her lips, she turns her wet face to the night sky.

'At last,' she whispers.

Now she can get the stink off her body and with it the smell of roasted human flesh. There was a bar of soap in the estate agent's handbag. A small round thing from a hotel still in its pretty packaging. Strange what people carry sometimes. And there's cash and credit cards too.

The cold rain sends her naked stick-like body shivering.

She rubs soap all over, against her wrinkled skin, into every orifice, upon her hair, her pubics, rubbing it in, rubbing it deep to get the stink away.

To purify memories of slicing flesh, of dragging out intestines, of cutting bleeding meat into big chunks, of lighting a fire in the already burnt-out lounge and the spit, splatter and fat sizzling. How delicious and strange is that roasting aroma? The feel of hot meat in her palms, still red and bloody.

Even as she chews, the grease coating her tongue, she can still hear the agent whispering.

Your house is perfect.

Yes, yes, perfect for living in squalor. Perfect for killing you.

With her rain shower done, the old woman retreats into the house, draws knees to chest on that metal bed and allows the water to drip off. She is still shivering and she's not sure if it's from cold or memory.

But what memory? So many of them that they often scream circles in her head.

The rain dwindles to drizzle and eventually stops. Water drips from blood-like leaves. Much blood she has seen this afternoon.

And what of the bones and uneaten flesh? She was in no mood for burying them earlier nor does she want to bury them now. Perhaps in the morning.

The rats can have their feast.

With belly full, sleep crawls up her thighs and chest, nods her head and gently lays the old woman's body on the bed and soon she is snoring, naked to the world.

* * *

The old woman's eyelids flick open.

Flecks of sunlight creep upon the walls. A chirp echoes from the big tree and she knows it's not real.

But one thing is for sure. The police will come just like they did the last time in their grey uniforms and tired, grim faces.

So she gathers a few things and slips through the gate opening, glances back at that haunted house and fairy-tale garden. No trolls, ogres, nor memories can hold her and soon she is sighing and shuffling along the main road. Her thoughts are blown away by the whoosh of traffic toward the tree tops and the ever-peering condominium towers.

The agent's clothes, although over-flowing on the old woman's body, make her look decent enough. One hand carries a bulky plastic shopping bag whilst the agent's handbag is slung over one shoulder and when she catches the bus, no one gives her a second glance.

Leaning her forehead on the window, she gapes at the passing scenery.

She has not seen these sights in years. So many new things, like those numerous towers rising skywards. Her blood is pulsing and her bones are no longer weary.

'It's good,' she whispers, 'to be out in this world again.'

The man across the aisle wears earphones and does not hear this or her subsequent mutterings as memories drag her one way then another.

She gets off the bus, the bus driver making sure this fragile-looking grandma is safely on the pavement before switching the door close with its usual hiss.

She stares wide-eyed.

Back in the city and its endless rows of old shophouses.

She enters a bright modern café. She is by a window staring out, sipping black coffee, hardly believing she has left her house, her garden, that she's out in the world. A place she promised herself she would never return to.

The teenage waitress brings over a plate of waffles, vanilla ice-cream and mixed berries. The old woman is not hungry for didn't she have a feast last night, a rather meaty affair that still sits heavily in her stomach? But still she digs greedily into the sweetness, the richness, the crunchy and soft textures. When was the last time such heavenly tastes touched her tongue?

Then there he is. That boy, sitting opposite her.

His hair falls over his forehead, his face cherubic and eyes big and innocent.

'Hello,' he says. 'That looks yummy. Can I have some?'

She ignores him. He has visited her before, from time to time especially when her thoughts are unguarded.

The boy glances around looking confused. 'What are you doing here?'

The old woman shrugs and frowns. She pushes the plate to him. She has lost her appetite. But the boy just stares at the plate of sweet richness without touching it.

He raises one hand in the air and floats in around, slowly turning it this way and that like a kite.

Yes, a kite indeed.

'Where is it?' he whispers.

He came to her house a few weeks ago. She was sitting in her usual spot by the collapsed kitchen wall, surrounded by dead leaves and rubbish bags, looking for the odd rat to kill.

The forest-garden is buried in shadows. Yet still the boy runs in.

She wonders what has drawn him here until he excitedly points up at the tree top.

A white kite in the branches.

Its red tail a long ribbon fluttering in a light breeze as if trying to escape.

The boy is looking up, standing beneath a tree in a white T-shirt and blue shorts, and hasn't noticed her until she is stooped beside him with a shovel in her hands.

'My kite,' he says.

'Let me get it for you,' she croaks.

She looks down at him. He is perhaps five or six.

His blue plastic slippers is covered in specks of sand.

'Where are your parents?'

'On the beach. The string broke. It went so high.'

His eyes are big and innocent.

'And your kite flew here, so you chased after it?'

The boy nods.

'And you left your parents on the beach? They don't know where you ran to?'

The boy turns to look back at the street. He nods again, slowly this time, a worried expression on his face.

She smiles at him.

To reassure him that such foolishness has no consequences. Running from the parents indeed. Poor, silly thing.

'I'll just shake the branch,' she says and raises the shovel above her head and strikes it several times, shoving it from side to side.

Sure enough, the kite comes unstuck and drifts down to the leaf-covered earth.

The boy gives a yelp of joy and bends down to pick it up.

Without giving it much thought—for why should she?—she brings the shovel hard on his exposed head. There is a crunching noise and he collapses to the dirt. She strikes his head again and again, breath heaving, blood rushing through her limbs.

And now here they are again, in this café.

She glances out the window at the passing traffic. She turns back, but he is still there, sneering at that plate of sweet richness that she can now barely look at for everything good in her life eventually turns sour, rotten and bad.

'You killed me,' he says. His voice is flat and lifeless. Perhaps because he has already accused her of that many times and there is no venom left in it.

She nods. 'Roasted you in my living room. Your parents, all those people came from house to house, looking for you.'

'Why did you kill me?' the boy asks.

She ignores the question. She isn't even sure if she can answer it.

'I just told them I hadn't seen you. Simple as that. The police came later. I told them the same thing. No one even asked if they could come in to look around.'

She shakes her head and sips her coffee.

'I might even have let them. They would have found your small body in my burnt-out living room. Your head all bloody and battered. They would have taken me away and locked me up forever. Or given me the hang man's noose. Maybe that's what I really wanted.'

'Why did you kill me?'

She shrugs. 'Maybe because I could. Yes, I was hungry but not that hungry. That old couple only visited the week before with a shopping bag of groceries. I roasted you that night and you were so very tender, like lamb. Meat falling off the bone.'

She turns to see a young couple walking in. They wear office clothes and are busy on their phones.

The boy is gone. There is just the plate of waffles, the ice-cream all melted.

She knows he will return. And what of the agent? Perhaps she will visit too.

Your house is perfect.

Yes, indeed. That is what she'll say.

But your body wasn't. The meat was a bit tough and stringy. Yes, that'll be her reply.

And she can never go back to that perfect ruin of a house. The police are bound to search the neighbourhood and not so casually like they did the last time.

Two disappearances in a matter of weeks. Too much of a coincidence. She may be old but she still has her wits about her. They may think her senile and ready to be discarded but she is here, making things happen. Still places to go.

She pays at the cashier from the agent's wad of cash and shuffles out on the street.

She'll take the bus and leave.

* * *

She is in a budget hotel in a small town two hours away.

It is night.

Head on the pillow, eyes on the tiny room's black-stained ceiling. Outside lights blink upon the thread-bare curtains. The window air conditioner rattles and the noise of traffic and distant music is like karaoke from a coffin.

It is well past two in the morning and sleep has not found her. Instead there is a dark creature breathing on her face, its gnarled claw-like hands upon her throat. She coughs and splutters. But it is just memory, ghastly and stinks of rotting flesh sharing her bed and squirming beneath the thin musty blanket.

She does eventually snatch some sleep but is jolted awake by a noise in the corridor. Shuffling footsteps followed by an echoey voice calling.

Over and over . . .

Calling her name. She is sure it is.

She gets off the bed, breathing hard, slowly opens the hotel room door, pokes her head out and blinks. A single light bulb barely lights up the hot, musty corridor.

The voice calls.

She steps out.

Two shapes stand at each end of the corridor.

The smaller one is the boy again. The taller one is the estate agent, her body chubby and her eyes wide, expressionless.

'Your house is perfect,' she says. 'I can still sell it for you.'

'I will never go back,' replies the old woman. 'And you are dead. You can't sell anything anymore.'

'Where's my kite?' says the boy. 'You must give it back.'

She turns to him. He is coming towards her, his arms raised as if asking to be hugged. Behind her, the agent stomps down the corridor towards her.

'Perfect house,' she moans. 'Perfect house. Let me sell it for you.'

Then the boy and the agent are upon her. Pulling her down, so that her face is on the carpet and she is screaming.

* * *

'Are you okay?'

The old woman stops shrieking and looks up from the grey carpet.

A man stands in shorts and a sleeveless T-shirt. He is in his forties, has thick eyebrows and wears round plastic glasses.

What has happened to the boy and the estate agent?

Gone. Just like that.

'Are you okay?' he says again. 'Are you hurt?'

She shakes her head and gets to her knees.

He helps her stand up. Her legs are trembling.

His room door is open and the light within brightens the corridor and sends shadows scurrying away. Her screaming has woken him up. Perhaps it has woken something in her too. But she doesn't know what that could be.

'Do you need a doctor?'

She shakes her head again.

She turns and shuffles back to her room.

Before she closes the door, she turns back to the man.

'Thank you.'

'You're welcome,' he replies.

Both doors shut and the corridor is empty again.

* * *

Later that morning, the man with the round glasses who works for a textile company almost drops his phone when he sees the old woman's photo on social media. Not sure of what to do, he finally calls the police.

Having checked out of the hotel well before they arrive, the old woman is waiting on a metal bench beneath a rattling ceiling fan at the bus station. She muses on how things hardly change for the bus is late when two uniformed men approach. They speak to her softly, almost apologetically, and she can only blink as they handcuff her thin limp wrists and haul her frail body into the police car.

Her plea of insanity is rejected by the courts. Perhaps there's too much publicity. Perhaps nobody cares for the mentally infirm. Perhaps it's politics.

Who can tell these days?

As she steps onto the gallows in the early morning light, bare feet on rough wood, she is glad that all of it, the pain, the confusion, the blood, the recriminations, can now come to an end, as it will eventually anyway. Just a question of when.

As the noose is fastened around her neck, she spies the top branches of lush trees just beyond the rough prison walls and wonders if a garden flourishes beyond.

Surely a lovely one. Its lawns and benches a place of rest for the tired and hungry. Abundant shade beneath the dense foliage from the burning sun. A haven to close one's eyes, even for just a moment, to forget this world and its sufferings.

And to just breathe.

Then she hears it. A single chirp that echoes brightly in her head.

Her body drops. The rope pulled tight.

Her bare feet swings just above the dirt.

A single sparrow takes to the air, circles the prison and like a forgotten dream vanishes into the distance.

No Ordinary Day

Jin Yi waited at the traffic lights.

Two vehicles and a bunch of motorbikes gathered in front of her sportscar and, in the rearview mirror, a line of vehicles gleamed metal in the afternoon sun.

It was no ordinary day for she just had an important meeting. Jin Yi was forty-two, had short hair and still looked good, glamorous even.

She grinned. The three men were truly captivated when she took them through the sales deck, giving them the rundown of her skin care business. She was about to thumb a message to one of them when . . .

The car window exploded!

She jerked back as glass sprayed on her hair and face. An arm shot through the smashed-in passenger window and plucked her handbag from the seat. She glimpsed black metal in a gloved hand, glimpsed stony eyes through the motorcycle helmet's face shield. She sat there stunned as his motorbike roared away.

The traffic lights turned green as the snatch-thief sped across the intersection. The cars ahead moved forward, giving Jin Yi just enough space for her red sports car to give chase and shoot around them.

* * *

Around the time the snatch-thief had spotted Jin Yi with her handbag on the passenger seat and began to tail her, Nasim had stopped his Yamaha outside the kindergarten gates. It was an Islamic one for he wanted his boys to be brought up as virtuous Muslims.

Clean-shaven, his slim body giving way to a slight paunch, he got off the bike, went it and collected his two sons.

Alif was four and Amran was five and both were dressed identically in a blue uniform in a long-sleeve top, tracksuit pants and blue sport shoes. Nasim opened the grey clam-shell shaped carrier box at the rear and slotted in their lunch boxes and drink bottles.

He placed helmets on both children, fastened the straps, then helped Amran get on the back of the motorbike. Nasim got on, reached out his arms for Alif, and helped him sit at the front.

Home was a twenty-minute ride away. With Alif in front and Amran at his back, he carefully weaved the motorcycle past several shops and made the turn towards the main road.

It seemed like any ordinary day.

* * *

Jin Yi's heart was pounding.

Adrenalin raced through her body. Bits of glass clung to her skirt, her hair. She had a cut on her cheek. She pressed a finger to it and saw blood. The passenger seat and floor mats were covered in broken glass.

Her car chased the snatch-thief up the slip road, onto the highway. Hot wind tore in through the broken window, tugging her hair. The supercharged engine shot her past other vehicles.

'I'm going to get you,' she snarled. 'Gonna run you down!'

The rider sped down the left exit. Seconds later, she made the turn, tyres screeching, into a narrow two-lane road with link houses on one side and shophouses on the other. The snatch-thief glanced back, his black helmet glinting alien-like in the sun.

With her handbag slung around his shoulder, diagonally across his body, he weaved around a couple of parked cars, his motorbike loudly snarling as if telling her to back off. They were both going too fast for this narrow, busy road. But, caught in the chase, neither seemed to care.

Jin Yi, at all cost, wanted her handbag back.

As she gave chase, Nasim pulled his Yamaha out onto the main road. He was a maintenance man at an office building and it had been a long day at work with lift problems yet again. His boys seemed tired too. Alif shifted restlessly on the seat as if something was wrong.

Nasim frowned, for up ahead beyond the canopy of trees, the sky had turned broodingly dark. Wanting to get home before the rain, he quickly weaved his bike between several cars.

From behind him, he heard an urgent honking.

Jin Yi kept hitting the car horn. She shot past several parked motorcycles and a group of food delivery riders waiting beside McDonald's. Life goes on, people still needed to eat, no matter whatever shit was happening.

The thief dashed into a turn, his motorbike snarling. She followed. For a moment he managed to pull away from her but, pressing hard on the accelerator, she soon closed that gap.

Dark clouds loomed over the flats and houses. But it made no difference to her chase.

What was her plan? Yes, it was to ram him. To nudge his rear wheel and send him flying. She didn't care if he got severely hurt or died. He shouldn't have robbed her. He would get what he deserved.

With his motorbike tilting sharply towards the bitumen, he shot past several cars. The on-coming lane was clear and she closely tailed him.

She was within nudging distance. Just as she felt the rapture of triumph blossom in her chest, rain splattered her windscreen.

An on-coming SUV flashed its headlights and she jerked the sports car back into her lane. As she did so, it skidded. She felt a jolt, heard a *clunk*, and a loud crash.

Her car spun, its rear struck the vehicle in front of her and came to a jarring stop as the front and side airbags inflated with an echoing hiss. The airbag material struck her forehead, wisps of her hair clung to her cheeks.

She was breathing hard, pressing her forearms on the grey nylon of the airbag. Shaken but unhurt.

Rain pounded against the car roof. She pulled off her sunglasses. In the side mirror, the thief sped away, tyres spraying water. He raised his fist triumphantly in the air. A punch in her stomach.

Then, with an awful worm-like feeling in her guts, she peered over the front airbag through the wet windshield to the crash scene hammered by drumming rain.

Her throat tightened.

Beside a grey car, a motorcycle lay flat on the road, its engine dripped a pool of black oil like blood into rainwater. The back wheel was twisted and its storage box flung open. Plastic containers, plastic bags and drink bottles were strewn about the bitumen.

A man with a yellow helmet lay like a broken thing on his side, clothes soaked, one leg over his fallen motorcycle. Ten feet from him, a small crumpled body was beside the rear of a delivery van. Rain splattered on the half-off helmet, the child's neck bent awkwardly. He was perhaps four or five.

On the other side, was an older child in the same blue uniform, body pressed on the wet bitumen like a rag doll, facing down, rain splashing his back, one shoe fallen off.

Small groups of people, unfurling umbrellas, got out of their cars. Was it to help or to look or to take photos for sharing? She wasn't sure. Didn't care.

The fallen man raised himself on one elbow, turned his head, lifted the safety visor and stared at her. Then fell back on the bitumen.

* * *

Nasim fainted after the crash. He had cuts and bruises. The doctor said something about a possible concussion. But he had no headaches. Just a ringing in his head that came and went like an evil birdsong.

But his two boys, none of the hospital staff would say where or how they were. Then two police officers, one older, one younger, came up to him in his hospital bed, their faces void of expression. The older one spoke.

Nasim flung his fists at the mattress, hot tears streaming down his cheeks.

'No, no, no . . .' he whimpered. 'Please! Tell me it's no true.'

But the police officer said the bodies were already in the morgue.

Nasim wanted to leap out of bed, fall to the tiled floor and curl up in agony. For he felt as though he'd been kicked in the stomach and his insides were bleeding.

He later found out that Alif had been thrown off the motorbike and his body struck the back of a delivery van breaking his neck. Amran though was in hospital for three days but succumbed to his injuries.

As for his wife, she climbed up a ladder, removed the ceiling fan. Then she tied a rope to the ceiling hook, wound it around her neck and stepped off the ladder.

Nasim managed to return to work for a few days and it may have been the best thing for him. But his nights stayed sleepless, alone in the flat, staring at the shadowed ceiling, the walls pressing in, not believing how the world could carry on after what had happened.

He nightly dreamt of his two boys, white sightless eyes peering from the foot of his bed, coldly whispering, gesturing with tortured fingers, words garbled.

When he wasn't weeping for his dead family, he scrolled miserably through his phone searching for that woman, trying to discover where she lived.

* * *

Nasim stopped at the guardhouse.

He presented his ID and, with a visitor's pass, rode into this mansion-filled gated community and parked two houses from hers.

His canvas bum bag hid a knife and was slung over one shoulder. Anyone would guess he was a handyman. Tiny flats or ridiculously big houses, they all needed to be maintained.

He peered through the ornate gate, then glanced around. No one on the roads, houses or gardens. All deserted. The rich liked it that way. CCTVs peered from each house but he didn't care.

He bit his lip. It was time to make things right. Whatever the cost.

He climbed the gate then hurried past the front garden to the back of the house. The woman's home was bigger than the others. Better looking too.

Rich people seemed to get away with everything. And this woman was richer than most.

He hid there beside the swimming pool, in the shadow of the gazebo, sitting beside the drain against the wall. He would wait till dark for darkness was now his friend, enshrouding him in its cold misery. He put his hand into the bag and hefted the knife handle. This would make things right. Just had to be patient.

While Nasim waited, Jin Yi was in the kitchen.

Even though more than a week had passed, the accident flipped over and over in her head, working out its imaginary permutations.

If only she didn't give the snatch-thief chase. If only it didn't rain. If only she didn't turn back into her lane so quickly and strike the motorbike. If only that bastard didn't steal her handbag.

These thoughts, like hungry crows, circled her head endlessly, their mournful cries echoing through her. It was her stupid fault.

The two boys died. The mother killed herself too. She shook her head and felt a dull ache in her stomach.

She prepared a simple meal and ate alone on a large glass dining table. When she was done, food half-eaten, she washed the dishes and wandered upstairs to her bedroom.

She lived alone after having fired her maid for stealing. The house had six bedrooms and a lounge like a luxury hotel lobby but she mostly used just the kitchen and her bedroom. This was a trophy house she long realized, its sprawling spaces hardly stepped in.

After night had fallen, Nasim used his elbow to break the sliding door glass, expecting a screaming alarm and security guards to rush over sirens blaring. But the alarm was faulty and had been turned off years ago.

This was it. No going back now.

Switching on his phone torch, he entered the house. There was a cut on his arm and shards of glass lay at his feet. He licked off the blood and made his way through the lounge into the dining room and kitchen.

No one around.

Where was she? He would find her and she would understand pain and grief and all the misery life can bring.

Silently he climbed to the next level and found five locked doors. He guessed they were bedrooms. Hers had to be on the next level.

He climbed the stairs, the shaky glow from his phone torch leading the way up to a large door.

This was surely her bedroom. With an ear to the timber, he heard television sounds. He quietly pushed against it but it was locked.

Damn it!

He felt blood rush into his face. But no . . . he would keep control. Stay patient.

No, he wasn't going to try to break down the door. That would be utterly foolish. She would call the police and he would be arrested. But he wasn't going to give up so easily.

He crept back down to the lounge, picked a sofa amongst several and stretched out. In the morning she would come down.

Then he would kill her.

He struggled to sleep. He thought of many things . . . of how he would kill the woman . . . of his wife and boys . . . of whether coming here was the right thing to do. When sleep finally claimed him, hours later, he dreamt of his boys.

Beneath the glowing moon, he was sprawled beside his fallen motorbike with plastic lunch boxes and drink bottles scattered everywhere.

Two shadows shifted and scurried on the road. At first he thought they were dogs or cats, but then the moonlight fell on their bodies. The were his dead sons crawling towards him, helmets on, visors raised. He could hear their low breathing. As they closed in, he saw blood streaming down their lips, eyes glowing white, eyeballs missing, mouths opening and closing, whispering.

We kill. We kill. We kill.

Cold hands touched his face.

They licked both sides of his cheek.

He quivered.

Then a blade flashed towards his throat.

He shrieked.

The nightmare tore him from sleep.

From far away echoed the call to prayers.

Was it telling him to not do this? To leave before it was too late?

He lay on the sofa, thoughts in turmoil, breathing hard.

* * *

As usual, Jin Yi woke at six.

For a change, since the day of the accident, she felt refreshed after a night's sleep.

She did her routine yoga stretches followed by a workout using several light weights.

Her concentration was much better and she could focus on her breath without the crows circling her head, crying out what she should and shouldn't have done. Telling her that it was all her fault.

Then she had a shower, slipped on a silk dressing gown and made her way down to the dining room and into the kitchen where she put the kettle on.

She was determined to have a good day. To let the past go. It wasn't going to keep hold of her and suffocate her with guilt.

As she was stirring her coffee, she heard a noise.

She turned.

The mug fell from her hands and shattered.

No, this couldn't be. Not here!

'W-Who are you?' she gasped.

But she already knew who he was.

Nasim.

The man she had knocked down. The man whose two boys and wife were dead.

Except Nasim didn't look like the man she had seen that fateful day. A scraggly beard covered his face and his eyes were wild. He looked ten years older.

Her face went cold.

A large knife gleamed in his hand.

'It . . . it was an accident,' she blurted. 'I'm so so sorry for what happened.'

'Yes, I know you're sorry,' he hissed. 'I know it was an accident. But it was because of you, what you did that caused it all. My dead boys. My dead wife.'

'I should never have chased after the snatch-thief. It . . . it was my pride. It was the adrenalin. It suddenly kicked in and I had to chase him.'

'So you're blaming your adrenalin?'

'No, no, I'm not. It's my fault. But you don't need to do this.'

'What do you think I want to do?'

'Kill me,' she whispered.

Nasim nodded.

He took no relish in what he was about to do. It was something he decided that had to be done. A natural consequence of all that had happened. A natural flow of things. He didn't hate this woman. But she had to die. Then he would kill himself and all this sadness, all this heartache, would come to an end.

'Please don't do that,' she pleaded, throat throbbing. 'I have money.'

Then, despite his intentions, he noticed the loose silk dressing-gown soft against her slim body, the material that accentuated the shape of her breasts. Her legs were thin and pale and one smooth thigh revealed by the slight parting of silk gleamed like a delicious promise. He just had to slice the pink silk belt and she would be naked.

He felt a stirring below.

Something he didn't think he could ever feel again. A something that was most unexpected. He was going to kill her and be done with it. Done with life. But now there was this something else. This complication.

'I don't care about your money.' He pointed the knife at her throat. 'You will go upstairs now, to your bedroom.'

As Jin Yi climbed the stairs, she heard his breathing and could smell his sour body odour trailing behind her.

'Hurry up!' he hissed.

She quickened her pace, knowing that each step led her closer to her death. She didn't want to die. But there was no way out. Maybe this was how she was going to pay. Maybe she deserved it for the stupidity of what she had done.

She pushed open the door and entered her bedroom. Nasim followed.

Cool air-conditioner air breezed over his face. A scent of womanly perfume hinted at flowery promises.

Her bedroom was huge, twice the size of his entire flat. A white wardrobe stretching on one side was maybe forty feet long. On the other side was a spa bath, toilet and shower.

A king-sized bed, the tumult of quilt and pillows, waited at the far end.

'Get on the bed,' he said, his throat dry.

She turned to him, eyes wide, suddenly realizing what he wanted. 'Please . . . please don't. You don't want to do this. Your wife, your boys, they wouldn't want you to hurt me.'

For a second, his eyes softened, as if he found pity, as if he realized the madness in his actions.

'Please . . .' she whispered.

But then his eyes hardened. 'No . . . you can't sweet talk your way out of this. Get on the bed!'

She whimpered.

She turned to see her pillows flung all over and the quilt half kicked-off the mattress. Her magazines, files and business cards were scattered on the floor.

This couldn't be happening. One minute she was making coffee and the next she was about to be raped . . . then killed!

Her heart was pounding, her body trembling.

'Get on the bed!' Nasim snarled.

She crawled onto the mattress, breathing hard, trying to think of what to do. She turned to him and sat up, sniffled as she drew her knees protectively to her body.

'You don't have to do this,' she whispered, her voice quivering.

'Shut up,' he snarled.

His eyes were wild, face gripped with desire, throat throbbing.

'Now take off the robe,' he hissed.

She shook her head.

'Take the bloody thing off or I'll rip it off!'

'No!' she screamed. 'No, no, no!'

'You will pay! You will pay for what you did!'

He tore off his T-shirt and flung it across the room. He was about to unzip his trousers when something made him turn his head. That was when he heard it.

A thud.

His first thought was that there was someone else in the house. Someone staying in one of the locked bedrooms.

Another thud.

But as his eyes focused on the far wall, a dark, spherical shape bounced its way across the tiled floor. Slowly it came . . .

Thud, thud, thud . . .

Like a bowling ball, it bumped along the length of the wardrobe towards him. It skipped and spun, now like an oddly-shaped basketball, leaving a long red smear like paint on the white tiles, before rolling sluggishly . . . and stopped dead at his feet.

He gasped.

This . . . this was no ball.

Two eyes stared at up at him.

* * *

It was a severed head of a young man.

The curly, greasy hair fell about the oily forehead. There was a whiff of cigarettes and the smell of blood. The mouth was open as if he was about to voice a protest through dry cracked lips.

Even as Nasim's face went cold, he was aware that Jin Yi had come up behind him to stare at this loathsome thing.

'What . . . is that?' she whispered, eyes fixed hard on the object.

He glared at her. 'Can't you see it's a bloody head?'

'What the hell! How did it get here?'

'Don't know. But this is . . . evil.'

'Yes . . . *abah*,' came a voice.

Nasim glimpsed blue sports shoes and his eyeballs crawled upwards to fasten onto two short figures. One taller than the other, in tracksuit pants and long-sleeved shirts.

Still wearing safety helmets, they slowly raised the visors to reveal pale, swollen faces. Not dripping blood as in his nightmare, but still their stony, dead expressions, their white sight-less eyes sent an awful chill through him.

'Allah!' he whispered. 'Amran. Alif!'

His knife fell, the blade clattering on the tiled floor.

Eyes swelling with tears, he shook his head. 'No, this . . . this can't be real.'

We kill. We kill. We kill.

They whispered.

'What? W-What have you . . .'

'We caught him,' Alif said in a dead voice. A voice resembling his son's voice but echoing from far away.

'Yes, we did,' Amran added. 'The thief was sitting on the toilet messaging on his phone. We came through the wall. I cut his throat.'

Nasim wanted to leap forward to hug his sons. But those white, sightless kept him away and he knew their bodies would be icy cold. He had held their chilled bodies, their faces and necks in the hospital, in the morgue and wished that he was dead.

He knew that these two weren't his sons anymore.

They were the undead.

'We came back,' Amran's voice echoed.

Alif slowly nodded. Lips silently moving as if uttering some ungodly prayer.

'To kill that bad man,' Amran continued, raising one finger to point at the severed head. The greasy curly hair over the forehead and ears, dry cracked lips parted.

Nasim wondered if the man deserved to die. He was only a snatch-thief not a murderer. Did he need the money to feed his family or was it for drugs? Whatever the reasons his actions killed them. And now his boys had taken revenge.

But what about the woman?

Didn't she deserve to die too? For didn't she chase the thief and cause the accident?

With the snatch-thief decapitated, the debt surely had been paid.

Suddenly, it was as if dust had been blown from his eyes.

He was a fool to come here!

What madness had made him break into her house to kill her? To even want to rape this woman?

His sons had saved him from himself, from his vile, senseless revenge. He could never forgive himself for this terrible sin. Whatever had happened, had happened. It was not her fault.

He looked up to thank them but they were gone.

Just like that. Not a word of goodbye. He wished he told them that he loved them. That he missed them so badly.

But he had to leave now. He would apologize to Jin Yi and flee. Where to, he didn't know. He would try to continue with life, find a way to . . .

His head was suddenly jerked back. He gasped for breath.

His body was yanked back, falling backwards on top of Jin Yi who gripped the pink belt from her dressing gown so tightly around his throat that it felt as though her fingers were being amputated.

She pulled harder still. From her bared teeth, her breath gushed animal-like.

Laying on top of her, his naked back pushed against her breasts, he struggled for air.

He kicked out repeatedly, one foot knocking a pillow to the floor.

She pulled the belt tighter and tighter, breathing hard. Sweat streamed off her face. The heat of his struggling body was on hers, smelling his sour body odour as his bare sweaty flesh quivered and strained against her.

He tried to scream but only managed a guttural rasp.

Surprised at how strong she was, he desperately tried prizing the choking belt free but his fingers strained uselessly. He struck behind him with fists and elbows, but they were glancing blows and most only struck the mattress.

'Now you will die,' she hissed. 'How dare you come here to try to kill me!'

He wanted to cry out that he was sorry but as he hopelessly struggled, blackness darker than night smothered him. Eventually, his limbs stopped protesting, and as a final spasm shot through his body, his head fell to one side.

She held his limp body against hers long after she knew he was dead, sweaty skins bound together. Finally, she released the belt from his neck and pushed his body off the bed.

She couldn't believe it. What had she done?

Crawling forward to the foot of the bed, she dropped her head on the mattress and closed her eyes. She had killed, killed a living person. With her own bare hands.

With eyes closed, tears ran down her nose and cheeks. She wiped them on the bed sheet and slowly sat up.

'No,' she whispered.

She had forgotten the severed head. It had left a long streak of blood on the white tiles like a surrealist art piece. The dead eyes stared as if mocking her. The greasy hair curled over the forehead and ears, cracked lips parted in a silent snarl.

'I finally caught you, you bastard,' she whispered. 'But . . . what am I going to do?'

She turned to see Nasim's corpse on the floor beside her mess of magazines, files and business cards. His eyes bulged. Mouth open so that she could see his tongue and teeth and a couple of dental fillings.

'I need to get rid of you,' she whispered. She glanced back at the curly-haired head. 'And you too.'

She knew someone who knew someone. In business you had to have backups, people who did dirty work if needed. You never knew when you might need such help.

'But the guardhouse . . .'

Nasim's entry would have been recorded. The police would trace him here.

'No, I have to call the police.'

The words spilled out with dread. Self-defence, that's what she'd say. He came to rape and kill her but she had instead killed him.

She nodded. 'Yes, he turned away from me just a moment. So I strangled him, officer. That's what happened.'

She glanced at the decapitated head.

'I'll just throw you in the dustbin. You should never have stolen my handbag.'

She got out of bed, stared out of the window and sighed.

This was a day she would struggle to forget.

It was certainly no ordinary day.

Administrator Number One

He's sleeping now. A short doze after sex as always.

Mouth slightly open. A deep deliquescent breath. The stink of garlic and cigarettes from a half-open, cave-like mouth.

Now all I have to do this night is to slip these tiny geckos, one by slimy one, into that waiting ear. They're no common house lizards. I have six of these tiny red reptiles, big heads, bulging black eyes, quarter the size of a common gecko.

Should I tell you how I got them?

Buying creatures that can slither down the ear canal and chew their way up the auditory nerve into the brain is not easy nor cheap. I had heard whispers of such creatures as a young girl in my village surrounded by paddy fields, rubber estates and piercing insect noises. The old ladies nattering on tattered woven mats beneath limp coconut trees said that such evil creatures can only be found in secret jungle groves inside rotting trees near murky water.

So now, in a town surrounded by palm oil plantations and dissected by an expressway, I asked around in a quiet voice to wizened women squatting on the dirt beneath weather-stained shophouses, across from the bustling wet market. Shadowed leathery faces who might know of such things, people you don't notice, those that lurk at the edge of our humdrum tech-addicted world. So now I have them at last, slithering about in a slimy dreadfulness in this trembling plastic box.

Ah, waiting so very eagerly, to tunnel down the ripened floppy ear of Administrator Number One.

* * *

A syringe floating toward the swelled artery, the needle glinting like a promise upon his skin. I injected the man.

He was in his mid-twenties, about my age, had freckles on his cheeks and hair down to his shoulders. He lay face down on the examination table. Grinning, eyes teasing, he had declared earlier that he preferred the jab in the buttocks. Then he quietly laughed. Half-embarrassed.

As soon as I withdrew the needle, I knew something awful had happened. He frowned, turned over, gazed at the ceiling and shivered, in a spasm that went from feet to chest. His mouth opened and gasped for air.

I turned around and stared at the vial on the metal tray. At the remaining drop of transparent liquid, its meniscus clinging like poison to the glass, my jagged shadow in its oily reflection. I stared at the white label.

'The wrong meds,' I whispered. 'Shit . . .'

I slid the rattling syringe on the metal tray as if it was a venomous snake, coiled and ready to strike.

No matter what the medical intern did, the patient was dead eleven minutes later. His neck craned towards the wall as if he couldn't bear the sight of me—eyes closed, hair falling across his forehead, lips drooping and lifeless.

The head nurse was in the treatment room, leaning against a wash basin, a finger waltzing through a tablet screen. She glanced up as I shut the door.

'Yes?'

'It . . . it was me.'

'What do you mean?'

'It was my fault. I . . . I gave him the wrong meds. He was allergic to that one. It was in his file. I did see it but . . .'

There it was: the awful, awful truth, hanging there in the barely cool air-conditioned air.

'You forgot? Or it just didn't register in your stupid head?'

I shrugged. It could have been either.

'You better sit down,' she muttered. 'Wait here till I get back. Speak to nobody about this. Nobody.'

Then she left the room, shutting the door behind her.

I sat on a chair beside a table that had a blood pressure monitor and a stethoscope. Equipment that seemed so irrelevant, so useless now. The minutes dripped by and not even the myriad worlds within my phone could hold my attention.

She returned and nodded grimly at me. 'The Head Administrator wants to see you.'

'Now?'

'Yes. Now. Go!'

So I dashed down the corridor of hurrying medical staff, weary patients and hushed voices, my mind numb. I went past the nurses station, ignored a lab technician who nodded at me in his stained white coat and into a crowded lift, my heart thumping, chest tightening.

I scurried past the lobby, its plastic chairs filled with rows of despondent patients clutching queue numbers, and out into the hot sun, where cars were parked and men mingled at the hawker stalls as if it was a day like any other, then into the next building and into a small disinfectant-smelling lift.

The Head Administrator's office was on the top floor. There were three other Administrators on the level below, so we all referred to him, the top man, as Administrator Number One.

Biting my lip, I knocked twice, heard a sharp voice call out and shuffled into the dim light of his large office. The air was musty and stale.

I shivered in my uniform. I didn't know if it was from the cold air conditioning or fear. At the far end, past the ageing leather sofa set and coffee table covered in dark glass, was a large timber desk filled with towering papers.

Administrator Number One had the habit of twitching his nose which made his thick plastic glasses bob up towards his mess of grey hair.

I told him who I was.

'Terrible, terrible thing,' he gushed, staring up from a plastic file, eyes carefully scrutinising me. With his striped office shirt pulled tight against his chest, a silver pen stood like a weapon in his breast pocket.

He scratched his ear lobe then stroked his tie as if wiping dirt off them. 'Very, very bad.'

'I'm so sorry, sir,' I said, bowing my head, wishing that none of this was happening.

He slowly nodded. 'Big trouble for you. Big trouble for all of us.'

I bit my lip and felt like weeping.

'You can never work again, you know. At any hospital. Not even as a cleaner.'

I swallowed. Tears swelled behind my eyes. I blinked them away.

'Sit down,' he ordered.

I slowly pulled a chair and sat, perched at the edge of the seat, wondering what was going to happen now. I stared at the towering piles of paper, the back of his laptop, a drug company's calendar, while a chill crept over my heart.

He narrowed his eyes. 'I may have to report your negligence to the police. Maybe you will have to go to prison.'

Tears spilled down my cheeks. I pulled out a tissue from the pocket of my pants and wiped them away. I could hardly breathe.

He said nothing but just stared at me as if I was an interesting specimen. Like a virus that didn't know how to mutate.

I couldn't believe this was happening. Just one stupid mistake was all it took . . .

'Please don't, sir,' I whispered.

He nodded. 'Maybe, maybe we can fix this problem.'

'How, sir?' I sniffed. 'How can we do that?'

His eyes gleamed. 'Maybe I can pay some people. Officials, certain directors, higher up. A sort of compensation. Then I won't need to make a report. There'll be no autopsy, no investigation. It will save you a lot of trouble and you can continue working here like before.'

'Like . . . like before?'

'Yes, like it never happened. But you need to *pay*. For the problem to disappear. That's always the case. I'm sure you understand. We all must pay for the wrongs we do.'

'How . . . how much, sir?'

He brightly grinned. 'Come, come over here. Bring your chair over. We can sort this out now.'

I got up, awkwardly wheeled the office chair over the carpet to his side of the desk and sat down. He swivelled his chair to face me. His belly was bulging. His skin greasy and his face dotted with dark acne scars. He smelled of stale cigarettes and something else which I wasn't sure of but didn't like.

'You will do this. Then I can fix the problem for you.'

Nose twitching, setting his glasses quivering up and down, he shifted the laptop on his desk so that I could see the scintillating blue screen.

'Now, which bank do you use? I need to see if you have enough money.'

I told him, he tapped the keyboard and the bank's website filled the screen.

'Username and password?'

'Why?'

He turned to me, eyes hard.

'You want this problem to go away?'

I nodded. I had no choice. I needed to protect myself. I didn't want to go lose my job or go to jail.

'Username and password. Now.'

He slid the laptop towards me.

I swallowed. Then keyed in the details.

He craned his neck. He paused for a moment, then pointed at my bank balance. 'That should be enough. Just about.'

I'd been saving for more than a year but with my phone beeping the security codes and a few clicks all my savings disappeared.

My bank balance dropped. Fell into a void. As if those numbers never even existed. Gone, just like that.

'Good,' he said. Then I felt one thin hand stroking my back, gently tugging my bra strap, then sliding down towards my buttocks. 'You can get back to your post now.'

'Thank you, sir,' I gasped and hurried out the office.

I stood shaking in the lift, tears rolling down my cheeks.

And so there was no enquiry. No autopsy. Just a fake report that said that the patient was given the correct medication but died of an undisclosed allergy. That was it.

I kept my job.

The mistake was easily hushed up. The hospital's reputation remained intact.

But I'd taken a man's life. A young man whose life was just beginning. He was a junior systems analyst with two young kids. His family would have been devastated.

I continued my work but I could never forget the image of our staff wheeling him away that afternoon, a green sheet over his body.

A numbness like a shadow followed me through the day. I didn't want to think of his corpse, of what I'd done. I just had to carry on working and perhaps, over time, I could forget this terrible, most shameful event in my life.

I figured that I would never need to see Administrator Number One again but, to my surprise, he summoned me a week later. In a panic, thinking that the truth was going to come out, I dashed over to his office.

He was standing, a collared white shirt over his plump body, not wearing a tie, hands on his hips when I came in.

'Sit down,' he said, gesturing to the leather sofa.

I sat down. The sofa seemed unnaturally soft and smelled musty,

He stalked over to me, sat down, his lips curling into a large grin.

'Are you well?' he asked in a thick, husky voice.

I nodded.

He moved closer so that his knee touched my thigh. I shifted away, forcing myself to smile at him so he wouldn't be offended.

He licked his lips. His tongue seemed unnaturally large and pink. 'We have things to talk about. To make sure this problem doesn't come back.'

I fixed my eyes on the coffee table's dark glass top, at the watery shadows within the shadowy reflection, wondering what Administrator Number One wanted.

It became all too horribly clear when he placed one hand on my knee, slid it along my thigh and up inside my uniform to cup my breast.

* * *

The realization crept up on me, like a haze being lifted from my mind to reveal an absolute certainty, that Administrator Number One must die.

I've been meeting him at a house, at least twice a week, at the far side of town. He would be there greeting me at the door in his white collared shirt, pen sticking out of the pocket, pink tongue licking his lips and ushering me upstairs.

There was a large bed there, the only furniture in the dusty house. So there I do everything he wants. Every position he can think of.

The thought of him touching me turns my inside cold. Tightens my stomach so that I want to moan in horrid disgust. Mostly with myself for allowing this to happen.

But I can't have the file re-opened. I don't want to end up in jail. I made a mistake. One single, stupid mistake.

Now I'm paying for it. I am his slave. Perhaps for the rest of my life.

So I must do something!

I try excuses. My vagina hurts, I plead, and cannot have sex. My period has come. But he doesn't care and carries on regardless.

I tell him that I need to leave, perhaps find work in another town or even a remote village. But he won't let me go. I say my mother suspects something as I'm hardly home now.

'So what?' Dark eyes gleaming, spectacles throbbing. 'Want me to re-open the file? Want to go to jail?'

I shake my head.

'Good. Now take your clothes off. Slowly . . . very slowly. Now take those panties off. Yes . . . like that . . .'

Even as I slip them off, I know I have no choice. I have to kill him.

How can I do it? Do I have the guts? And what if I'm caught?

But I cannot live like this anymore. I must do something. Anything.

Then I remembered the stories. Of geckos that kill.

* * *

He lets out a soft snore.

I almost drop the small white plastic box containing the red lizards. I had only seen the squirming reptiles once: this morning in a battered Toyota. The woman in the driver's seat wore a loose black dress with white stains. She was perhaps in her sixties, with grey hair tied in bunch, a thin face, dark complexion and a large brown birth mark on her neck. In a low obsequious voice, she told me the price of each gecko and said I needed six.

'But why? Isn't one enough?'

'No, no, young lady, of course not. It doesn't work that way. Four will kill for sure. But you need six . . . just in case. One or two will just cause madness, unless that's what you want.'

Perhaps madness, I figured, was enough for Administrator Number One. She was asking a lot of money for just one gecko. But I decided that I couldn't take the risk.

'But I know things are not so easy nowadays,' she whispered, lips curled into a dry rust-like grin. 'So I'll charge you just for five, young lady. Buy five, get one free.'

I blinked at her. 'Will it be a painful death?'

'Yes, very.'

Good. I wanted him to die in agony.

'So you will take all six?'

'Yes, all . . . all of them.'

She nodded her head in sly approval. 'You won't regret it, young lady.'

She slipped the slimy things one by one from a metal tin into a small yellow plastic box I had passed to her, counting off each one in a soft but clearly excitable voice as each one slipped in, guided by her quick, artful fingers. I watched in awe at their flicking tails, short legs making tight swimming-like motions, eyes bulging black, each lizard a quarter the size of a house gecko.

'See how hard they're wriggling?' she said. 'Very healthy, these ones. I don't cheat you.'

I had no idea what a healthy gecko looked like but I wanted them vigorous and strong so that they could do their job. Their lovely killing.

She clicked the lid shut.

'They'll live for two days without feeding. You don't even need to give them water.'

I nodded, passed her the money and left with my box of lizards. I got into my car and glanced back, but the Toyota was already gone.

My new pets wouldn't be hungry long. They would feed tonight.

I met him at set days during the week at that house surrounded by rows upon rows of parked cars and other houses. Always at a set time after dinner. He was an organized man. That made him not only a good administrator, but Administrator Number One.

So here I am in the master bedroom that's up the staircase fronting the house, the plastic box sweaty in my hands. Sitting cross-legged, the thin blanket pooled around my naked body, I feel myself hardening with the certainty of purpose. If it wasn't for the humming window air con, I would be able to hear insects calling out their encouragement outside. If it wasn't for the curtains, I would be able to see the lights from the distant port and perhaps even a container ship slipping in death-like upon the black waters. If it wasn't for this cheating, greedy Administrator Number One, I wouldn't be here ready for murder.

I watch his sleeping body, the rising of his chest with each breath he takes. I wait a moment and I am almost ready.

My plan, it is simple enough. Open the lid slightly, then carefully tip the box over his one ear and watch the geckos disappear down his ear canal. For isn't that what they do in the jungle's rotting depths, leaving a clutch of dead monkeys hanging from trees? He would be dead within a minute. Then I'd slip back on my nurse's uniform and leave the house, driving off at a speed that draws no attention. And my problems would be finally over.

I had injected the patient and killed him by accident, by my own negligence. But I will kill this wretched man with a coldness that trickles up my spine and into my breasts. He even has his head turned slightly away, presenting his left ear, even making a gentle slope for the geckos to slither down. I know I have to do it now or I won't ever be able to do it.

I push my hair back and lean towards him. His teeth are stained yellow from cigarettes. A couple of hairs poke from his nostrils like broom bristles. The acne scars are darker in this dim light that creeps from the bathroom where sits a dustbin and a used condom.

I hover the corner of the box over his ear and slowly, holding my breath, click the lid open then quickly push it back against the lip of the box, using my thumb to put the pressure on, to stop them from escaping. There is darting movement within, a shuddering excitement at their imminent release or perhaps a realization that it is time to feed, sending the box almost toppling from my hand.

Administrator Number One stirs.

I freeze. A drop of cold sweat drips down my temple. My heart is pounding even as I fight to stop my hands from shaking.

He grunts. Clears his throat.

Goes quiet then falls back into that noxious liquid-like breathing.

I move the box so that it is almost touching his ear then, slowly, I take my thumb off and open the lid a crack. Almost immediately, the first shadow darts out wriggling out of the box, tiny and slimy and red in this half-light. It falls, feather-like upon Administrator Number One's ear lobe. It pauses there for a second, its head arching towards me, the large eyes almost enquiring about why it's here at this place at this time, before scampering and disappearing down the ear canal.

As if this was what it was waiting for, the next gecko darts out of the box and lands lightly on the ear lobe. It flicks its tail twice and slithers into the ear. Then out falls the next one.

And so, one by one they emerge and vanish!

I almost giggle with joy and triumph as they drip out like clots of squirming blood.

My eyes dart to the ceiling, almost expecting stars to appear in celebration. My heart, how it soars!

My plan is working!

All of them, each wriggling red reptile, all six of them, have squeezed hungrily into his ear.

But Administrator Number One does not move.

Why, why not?

Perhaps the geckos are not doing what they're supposed to do? They should be biting their way up his auditory nerve by now, deep into his brain and feasting on his soft grey tissue. But he just lays there breathing that liquid-like, satisfied breath.

Perhaps they've just gone to sleep in that narrow ear tunnel? The thought of that makes me want to shriek in frustration.

I click the lid back on and shove the box back into my handbag on the bedside table. I slip on my uniform, fingers struggling with the buttons, breath ragged, eyes not leaving him.

Still he lays there in his after-sex sleep, unmoving in his dream world.

I know I've been tricked.

These geckos aren't the correct ones. They don't kill. They don't leave monkeys hanging dead from trees. Maybe such killer geckos don't even exist. Just tall tales to frighten young children!

That damn woman cheated me. Took my hard-earned money and gave me lizards that do nothing.

I have to leave. I cannot stay. It doesn't matter if he finds me gone when he wakes up. He'll be angry but I'll make up some excuse.

I grab my bag and creep towards the bedroom door, biting my lip, trying to contain my disappointment.

But there's a rustling of the blanket.

Slowly I turn and what do I see?

His bulky shadow looming above the bed.

Where the hell are you going?

I thought he would shout. But he doesn't.

Instead Administrator Number One is sitting bolt upright in bed, his grey hair curling over his forehead. The light from the bathroom illuminates his shivering, contorted face, his trembling naked body.

His lips move. Wordless at first The tongue slips in and out. Then I hear the muttering, something about angels and thieves and a country of dead people.

'What, what are you saying?' I whisper.

He rises to his knees, the blanket falls off his plump naked body.

His eyes blink, then slowly open. The whites of the eyes are pink, reminding me of the red geckos with colour leeched from them. He stares right at me—no, right *through* me.

'My glasses . . .' he mutters. 'Where the hell . . .'

His jaw drops. His eyes wide. One ear quivering.

'Ahhh . . . my head!'

His hand reaches for one side of his temple, the fingers claw-like as if he wants to gouge out his brain.

His cheeks tremble. The tongue flops out, bigger than ever.

Then he screams.

An echoing scream filled with horror and pain that makes my heart go cold.

He falls off the bed, grey hair flying, hands grabbing at empty air as he shrieks, a sound of a man dying as if he is being pierced by a thousand fiery needles. He falls with a loud thud on the tiled floor.

I stand paralyzed staring at the naked squirming body, blood dripping out his ear and streaming down his neck and pooling on the floor. His mouth is wide open in a soundlessly scream.

I feel nothing. Just a resounding satisfaction.

Then he uncloses one eye and his mouth opens as if gasping for breath.

He slowly whispers 'I . . . I love you'.

'Fuck off' I say and kick him in the head.

Then I leave.

* * *

I bolt out the room, hurry down the stairs and flee the house, not even shutting the front door behind me, and drive home at high speed.

I play the music loud but nothing can erase the image of Administrator Number One falling off the bed and dying on the floor, blood leaking from his ear.

And his stupidly disgusting *I love you*.

I arrive home.

'You're back early,' says my mother who is washing a frying pan.

I ignore her, scurry to my room, lock the door, flop on my bed. I fling my handbag against the wall, bury my head under the pillow.

I want to scream and laugh all at once.

My mother is knocking on the bedroom door, calling me.

'What's wrong? What's wrong? Tell me?'

She keeps knocking and asking me if I'm okay.

I wipe tears of laughter from my eyes. I open the door, look into my mother's worried face and grin.

'Everything is fine, mother. Everything is good now.'

* * *

But no, no, no . . . everything is not good.

Everything's bad. Very bad.

Because a sound, a movement, has woken me. I open my eyes.

All is dark but for a slit of light coming in through the curtains. The stand fan is humming and rattling. Vehicles distantly drone on the expressway beyond the river.

It's hot and beads of sweat form on my forehead.

There it is again. An almost inaudible chirping.

What is it? A sound so cold no bird can make.

Then there's a tiny but unmistakable shape on the blanket. I almost didn't see it. It is slowly crawling up the blanket, over my elbow, towards me.

No, can't be!

What is it doing here? I dropped all six geckos down Administrator Number One's ear.

I counted all of them as they fell . . .

Or did I?

Was there one left? A shy one clinging inside the plastic?

It must have been hiding in the box in my handbag, just waiting to come out!

Before I can turn and strike at it, I feel the slimy thing dart up my shoulder, feel tiny cold feet scurry up my hair, upon my skull and onto my ear. I grab at it to fling it to the other side of the room but I already feel the cold slithering in my ear canal, its tail flicking against my outer ear before its whole body slips in.

I leap out of bed, bellowing.

My thoughts are in frenzy, my heart madly pounding.

I need to get it out!

I switch on the lights and search for something to poke it out with.

But what? And will I not only injure myself? Burst my ear drums or worse? But the gecko will do even more damage for . . .

There's knocking on my bedroom door.

'What's happening?' my mother calls out. 'Are you alright?'

'Yes, yes, It's fine!' I scream back.

But, of course, it's far from fine.

I open the door to see my mother's worried face.

I'm about to tell her that there's no problem and that she should go back to bed when I feel a hard pinch within my skull.

Then a throbbing that pierces the left side of my temple.

'No . . .' I moan, falling to my knees. 'No!'

Tears spill down my cheek.

My mother tries to help me up. 'What's wrong? Are you . . .'

I hug her tight. I never want to let her go.

'I . . . I need to tell you something, mummy. Before it's too late.'

'What . . . what is it?'

'I love you.'

'Yes, I know that already.'

I nod. I keep nodding. Can't stop it.

Perhaps the gecko is nodding too.

The hot needle is now piercing deep into my skull.

I scream and fall to the floor.

My mother leans over me, trying to help me up, but darkness, blacker than black, engulfs us.

* * *

I'm sitting cross-legged, a mannequin in bed.

A deep throbbing in the left side of my skull. It comes and goes. Sometimes it's like ice, sending a shiver through it. Sometimes it's a burning from the pits of hell.

There's an infernal itching in my ear.

I need to scratch it, rip flesh to shreds, but I refrain.

The doctors have come and gone. Come and gone, nodding and whispering.

They tell me that my brain is damaged. Anatomically ruptured. Physiologically unsound. Causing prolonged bouts of delusion.

How wrong they are!

For my thoughts are so clear. Clearer than ever before.

A woman often checks on me. I pretend she's my mother. She seems so sad.

Please understand that I'm not insane. For could a mad, delusional woman comfort that woman the way I did? Even holding her hand and saying I love her?

No, I am not mad. Just enlightened. Super sensitive too.

So that the lights hurt my eyes.

And ants crawl my thighs. A cockroach feelers dance upon my big toe.

A gecko on my forehead. Tail swishing, red pendulum between my eyes.

Whispers sound like crackling skin, drift from the shadowed corners of my bedroom. But is it my bedroom? Is this not a hospital? Or a seaside hotel visited by blue mermaids, hair dripping with salty water?

I decide it's a hospital for nurses' footsteps echo down the disinfectant-smelling corridor. The clatter of instruments being wheeled.

Click, click, click on the tiled floor.

Beneath my bed he's whistling.

It's Administrator Number One. He wants to climb on the bed for sex one last time, his mouth drooling, his thick plastic glasses bobbing, eyes pink like the leeched out colour of the geckos. Blood leaking from one ear.

But I ignore him.

Control, demeanour is everything.

I've been behaving so well. Hiding my thoughts. Nodding at the right moments. Saying the correct things. Could a mad woman keep up such pretenses?

The doctors will soon discharge me, they said. Perhaps next week. Then I'll buy more geckos.

For they need to feed.

Karaoke Nightmare

'Thanks,' Aliya says, taking the bulky cardboard box from the delivery man.

She hauls it into the the lift, rides it up to the eleventh floor, then down the open corridor to the humming of vehicles and a view of the highway below. She unlocks the metal grille, opens the front door, kicks off her slippers and slides the box into her apartment.

Closing her front door, she hurriedly cuts the cardboard box open, slides out the item, discards the polystyrene, tears off the plastic and smiles.

Her portable speaker karaoke system has arrived!

Being hand-luggage sized and with two wheels plus extendable handle, the karaoke set begs to travel.

'Yeah, we can go on honeymoon together,' she says. 'Maybe to Bali or the Maldives. I don't need a man in my life.'

But she knows that's a lousy lie. She once had a serious boyfriend and wonders if she'll ever find another or will she end up as an old maid watching Netflix until she's a dried-up corpse.

She sighs and eyes the karaoke set as if it's a potential lover. Its entire front is one large speaker, a giant eye that only has eyes for her.

Wheeling her new-found friend over to the large-screen TV, she plugs it into an electrical socket, switches it on, slots batteries in and clicks on the wireless microphone.

'Hello, everyone,' she says. 'It's me, Aliya!'

Her voice comes through loud and clear. For a while she just stares at the large speaker whose giant dark-grey eye stares at her expectedly, perhaps keen to board AirAsia. But no, it can only stare back for one reason.

'I know, I know,' she sighs. 'But I cannot sing. Not to save my life or anyone else's. So why did I buy you?'

She grimaces at her new friend. She knows exactly why.

I want to sing well. I want it sooooooo badly.

Aliya loved singing as a young girl. She told her mum that she wanted to join a band when she grew up. She thought maybe a RnB group or a girl band or a solo career as a diva.

'There are so many other jobs out there,' her mother sighed. 'And a singing career is for people who can sing well. You're not so good at it. Anyway, it doesn't pay much. It's not a reputable job. Better to be a doctor or a lawyer or a millionaire YouTuber.'

There it was. The truth. Aliya couldn't sing. It was not that she couldn't sing well, she just sung *badly*. That's what her mum said.

Like a toad?

No, no, no. Surely her mother didn't say that!

At school, Aliya insisted on joining the choir.

'It's not for you,' her teacher, Mrs Lee said.

'Why not?' Aliya asked.

'Well, the truth is that you can't sing. You're always out of key. And your voice, well, it doesn't sound good.'

Like a toad?

No, Mrs Lee couldn't have said that either.

'But teacher, what do you mean my voice doesn't sound good?'

'Hmmm, actually, Aliya, it sounds . . . well, let's just say (*you sing like a toad?*) it'll make sleeping babies cry. Why not join the chess club or girl guides?'

So there it was. The truth.

She was sure she would get better if she practiced, and so the bathroom echoed with her voice as she ladled scoop after scoop of water from the big plastic bucket over her body through her growing years. Her baths took so long that all in her family complained.

Now that she had a good job, her own condo and her own real shower for non-stop crooning, her voice just had to be perfect.

But how wrong she was.

For just last week, it struck her like a hammer on her drunken skull.

* * *

Aliya really liked her friends. Even though the five of them were like a multi-racial soup, she sometimes wondered who the head chef was. And was he or she any good?

Kai was a cool Malay partying guy. Zin Yee was pretty, Chinese, and had her own online business. The other Chinese in the gang was SK, he worked in IT, was divorced and at thirty-two was the oldest amongst the gang. Finally, there was Ram, a Malayali, an overweight junk-food vegetarian, who worked in the family import business.

Aliya's father was Muslim Javanese and her mother a Christian Chinese. After their divorce, her mother brought her up as a Christian but at school she was cajoled into wearing a *tudung*. There was no running from her Muslim name, but still she yearned for free hair and to choose her own religion.

Now, hair flowing freely, she was glad to hang out with this diverse non-judgmental gang. They enjoyed not only meals together but outdoor activities too. But then, quite out of the bluest of blue, Zin Yee suggested karaoke.

The five of them met that evening and ordered two jugs of cold Tiger. The room was well air-conditioned and had cool, designer plastic seats attached to three multi-coloured painted walls.

With lights dimmed, they chose their songs.

Zin Yee, eyes brimming with excitement, went first with Taylor Swift.

Aliya's mouth fell open.

Zin Yee was always confident, wore expensive clothes and had designer handbags, but Aliya didn't realize that Zin Yee could sing, voice soaring and hitting each note perfectly.

Zin Yee hogged the mic for several numbers before SK's Jay Chou song came up. SK's voice though was like a tired wind on tattered sails driving a run-down yacht into jagged rocks. He seemed happy though, not caring how he sang.

Zin Yee came on again, singing Billie Eilish and Ram picked up the second mic to join her. Together they continued with Five for Fighting.

Kai went next with Maroon 5. Aliya liked his intelligent eyes and sense of humour. Except he didn't show much interest in her. She could tell Zin Yee liked him too from the way her eyes roamed up and down his muscular body.

Then it was Aliya's turn. Grasping the mic confidently, she would show that Zin Yee how to sing. Kai would be so impressed too. She was going to surprise them.

Hers was Mariah Carey.

As the lyrics ran like water across a scene of snow-covered mountains, Aliya wriggled her body and joyfully sang. Her every note perfect, her voice beautiful, soulful too.

Wasn't it?

Then why was Zin Yee sniggering? Why was SK frowning and blinking hard as if someone was pulling his ears?

Ram gulped his beer, fingers on his temple as if he had a headache. Kai was vaping and grinning conspiratorially at Zin Yee.

What was happening? Were they making fun of her singing?

She pretended not to see and instead just stared at the screen and sang. Her heart though was beating fast. Her mind in turmoil. She began to mispronounce the words. Even got some notes wrong. Her voice had become a sinking ship, being swallowed by the choppy waters of doubt, dread and disaster. She was drowning.

When the song thankfully ended, she heard laughter. Zin Yee's voice was the loudest, but others were giggling too. Only Ram was quiet, staring at her as if she were some kind of demon from hell.

She turned away, her cheeks hot with embarrassment, wanting to burst into tears. She dashed out of the door but not before overhearing Zin Yee say '. . . *like a toad* . . .' followed by everyone's uncontrolled chortling.

She fled down the corridor, scurried into the toilet, sat in the cubicle and wept. Wasn't she a good singer? She thought she was. All the practice she had done through the years was a bloody waste of time. She was a lousy, awful singer. How could she fool herself into thinking she was like Mariah Carey?

Going back to the karaoke room, tail between her legs, she was afraid to look them in the eyes. She refused to sing even though Zin Yee said they were just joking about her singing. Despite their pleading, Aliya spent the rest of the evening just drinking beer and getting drunk.

And the worse thing was that, at the end of the evening, everyone said they had so much fun that they were going to do it again.

Very soon.

* * *

The bitterness from that evening, that karaoke nightmare, is lodged like nails in her heart.

She stares at the big speaker.

All is silent except for a blower awfully droning in the garden below, sending fallen leaves to who-knows-where. She wonders if her singing is any better.

'There's no use us just staring at each other,' she says to the dark-grey metal mesh unlike a fly's compound eye. 'It's time.'

She slides the glass door shut.

Then she summons up YouTube on her TV, selects a Lady Gaga karaoke song and begins to sing.

But soon stops. She realizes one thing.

She sounds like a croaking toad!

Why didn't she know that before? No wonder everyone was laughing. She had been deluding herself all these years.

She wants to collapse on the floor and cry.

'Why did I buy this stupid machine? I just can't sing. What's the use of practicing? I've done that for so many years.'

But she wants to sing well. She wants to sing like Zin Yee. Better than her and wipe that stupid grin off her face!

She wants her friends to apologize for laughing. Maybe she can even capture Kai's heart with her voice. Maybe, just maybe, she can do that.

Then she blinks.

Why didn't she think about it before?

She types 'singing lessons' into YouTube.

The video she selects goes through a warm up. Explains the chest voice, mix voice, head voice, falsetto. Yes, she understands the principles.

An hour has passed. But she hasn't opened her mouth.

Shouldn't she start singing?

She backtracks to the vocal warm up section and sings the notes as the keyboard tinkles up and down the scale. How's she doing? She's not sure. The woman on the video with a Russian accent keeps saying 'Good job' but Aliya has no idea if she's doing well or if she's a croaking toad.

She needs feedback. She needs to know how she's doing.

As if her thoughts were being read by some unknown force, up pops and advert.

Master class singing lessons. One to one with a master vocalist instructor.

Yeah, but that's going to be massively expensive, she says to herself. She's about to click 'Skip Ad' when a voice says: 'What's more, the lessons are free. That's right, absolutely one hundred per cent absolutely free. No strings. No nonsense.'

Click to find out more.

What has she got to lose? And the lessons are free.

But part of her hesitates.

What's the catch? There's nothing free in this world. And why spend all that money on an advert only to give away lessons?

Sure the first couple of lessons will be free. Then she has to pay and pay big. But what can it hurt to have a look?

So she clicks the button which opens a web page.

She stares. The page is stunning. Beautifully designed.

In a decorative font, it reads:

The gift of a perfect voice will cost you nothing financially. What's more, you'll find your perfect voice in a miraculous twenty minutes. Just click 'Agree' to get started.

Aliya frowns. How can one get a perfect voice in twenty minutes? Has to be a scam. She knows she can't sing. A perfect voice in twenty minutes? No way.

But, before she can stop herself, she clicks 'Agree'.

This is it. Let's see what happens.

Up pops a congratulatory message.

She registers by entering her name and email address.

A man appears on her television screen. A handsome man in his thirties. He looks Korean with his fair skin, his neatly cut hair. He looks a bit like Jin from BTS except that his hair is greasy black.

His intense, mysterious, coal-like eyes look right into hers. For a second, they seem like the karaoke speaker, that one dark-grey eye, the metal mesh like a fly's compound eye, daring her to sing. Antennas flickering, mouth parts sucking.

'Hi,' he brightly says. 'My name is Air. Congratulations on joining this course that's going to change your life. I'll teach you to sing like a star. And guess what? It's only going to take you twenty minutes.'

Aliya stares at him, eyes wide. Her skin tingles with excitement.

He's so good looking too, his skin so smooth and pale. And his voice so soothing, confident, convincing. But how can she become a great singer in twenty minutes? Is this a dream? No, it can't be real.

Air grins at her. 'Can't believe it? Well, it's true. Absolutely one hundred per cent true. Or your money back. But wait a minute, it's a free course and you've been chosen. That's right, this course is only given to a select few, a *very* select few, to those who I know can make it. To those whose voice can be trained perfectly. It'll just take you twenty minutes. So are you ready?'

Aliya can't believe this is happening . . . But she wants to. And it's free. What's there to lose?

She nods desperately, even though she knows he can't see her, that this is just a video. But he seems to be talking right at her, looking deeply into her eyes.

'Great,' Air says. 'Now Aliya, all you have to do is follow my instructions . . .'

What!

Her mouth falls open. 'This . . . this isn't a video?'

Air leans forward, eyes bright. 'No, it's not, Aliya. I'm here talking directly to you, one to one. I'm your personal instructor and this is a private lesson. I'm going to make you a fantastic singer. Everyone is going to love your voice. You just have to follow my instructions, Aliya. That's all you have to do.'

Aliya blinks. 'W-What do I have to do?'

'Just listen to me, that's all. After our lesson you'll become one of the greatest singers in the world. If not the very best. But there's one thing stopping it.'

'What's that?'

'We can't have people remembering your old voice. The fact that you were a terrible singer. So those friends of yours from last week?'

How can he know about it? The karaoke nightmare.

Aliya can't believe it.

'What about them?' She swallows, her throat dry.

Air grins. It brightens up his face. He licks his lips.

'It's just a simple thing you have to do, Aliya. Just one simple thing and the whole world can listen to your wondrous singing. You just need to kill them.'

'No!'

* * *

But she did agree. And you would too, wouldn't you?

For after one single lesson, her voice no longer belongs to her. It belongs to the universe, it soars, dances and floats, every note filled with wonder and a delight that are beyond words.

'I can't believe it!' she gasps after she had finished the song. 'I knew I could sing well, but not like that. Not with this absolutely amazing voice.'

'You always had it in you,' Air says, eyes gleaming. 'I just had to bring it out. So simple if you know how.'

'Those bright flashes of light as I went up and down the scale. What was that?'

'That's my secret, Aliya. It connects your brain to your breath and vocal cords in a special way. Not just that, but it connects your brain to your soul and to the eternal universe. It makes you the best singer ever! Makes you angelic!'

Aliya nods excitedly.

Air leans forward. 'But this new voice of yours can't be shared with the world. No, not yet. There are four people out there who've recently heard your old voice. They can no longer be part of this world. You understand, Aliya?'

Aliya nods again.

Friends that made fun of her, laughed at her singing, were not real friends, were they? No, of course not!

'Yes,' she whispers, her throat dry, 'I-I do,'

'Good,' Air says, grinning magnificently.

Aliya frowns. 'But . . . but how do I kill them?'

'That's simple. I'll tell you what you need to buy. You just mix them in the right proportions. You'll end up with a white powder. You just need to slip it into the beer. They won't know a thing. They'll feel faint, collapse and fall asleep forever. So very simple. Will you do this?'

'Yes, of course, I will.'

'Good. When's your karaoke session?'

'In three days.'

'Good. That'll give you lots of time to prepare the ingredients.'

Aliya's heart skips a beat. For it is filled with dread.

* * *

Aliya waits nervously at the entrance of the karaoke centre.

Zin Yee appears and beams. 'Hi, Aliya!'

Despite the squirming in her belly, Aliya manages to grin back. 'Hi, Zin Yee!'

Zin Yee is wearing a pink dress, her hair has been recently dyed a light brown and she wears that bright-red lipstick.

'Hello!'

Aliya turns around to see SK eagerly approaching. He's so nice and polite that Aliya wonders if she can go through with it.

'Shall we go in first?' SK says.

'Come on, guys,' Zin Yee says. 'I can't wait to be a super diva.'

They pay the fee at the cashier's counter which doubles as a small bar then stroll down the corridor to the karaoke room. It's the same one as last week. Zin Yee hurriedly chooses her songs from the touch screen.

Alya almost feels sorry for her.

This is the last time you'll be singing.

But the thought of killing her, of poisoning all of them, sends a cold shiver up her spine. She knows though that she can't back out. With her new voice, they'll soon be lining up those recording records.

The door opens and a waitress brings in two jugs of beer and five glasses. She places them on the round table, condensation dripping down the sides.

Aliya's hand is trembling. She reaches into the back pocket of her jeans and fingers the small plastic packet containing the white powder. She has to slip the power into the jug of beer. Just has to wait for the right time.

Zin Yee is into her third song when Kai and Ram step into the room, big smiles on their faces.

'How are you, Aliya?' asks Ram, a mischievous twinkle in his eyes. 'Gonna thrill us with your singing again?'

Alya smirks. 'Sure, it's gonna be a big surprise.'

'Hey, leave the girl alone,' Kai quips. 'She's a great singer.'

Aliya nods at him. She's not sure if he's being sarcastic. Maybe they could have been a couple, perhaps if she had let her feelings show. But that didn't matter now. Nothing mattered.

Kai, SK and Ram choose their songs while Zin Yee sings Rhianna followed by Amy Whitehouse.

Soon everyone has had a turn on the mic. Everyone except Aliya. She says she can't sing because of a sore throat. Her eyes have hardly left the jugs of beer. One is empty. The other almost.

'I'll go order more beers,' she says to Ram.

'You can just press the button to call the waitress,' he says.

'Don't worry. I'm going to the toilet so I'll get more when I'm out there.'

She wanders down the corridor over to the bar area with the empty jugs and orders two more jugs.

The waitress fills them up from the dispenser.

Aliya stops her from taking the jugs to the room.

'I'm going back in. So I'll take it.'

'Okay,' says the waitress. She pulls out her phone and strolls away.

Aliya glances around. With no one looking, she quickly slips the plastic bag from her pocket, peels it open and drops an equal amount of powder into each jug. She swirls each jug around making sure the powder dissolves.

Then she takes the jugs back into the karaoke room.

Zin Yee is still crooning away. Her friends smile as she enters. For, after all, she is bringing cold beer. Condensation (*like tears?*) dripping down the glass jugs.

Aliya grins back even though a chill runs up her spine. With a trembling hand, she pours beer into the empty glasses, spilling some on the table.

They continue to sing, drink and occasionally dance and have a stupendously great time. That is until they start to stagger and collapse on the seats, on the floor.

Kai drooling, unable to balance himself, leans his head against Aliya's shoulder. She gently helps him sit down. His head bent over, mouth open, eyes death-like.

Ram is sprawled on the carpet, foaming at the mouth.

Zin Yee has collapsed on the far corner, vomit on her pretty pink dress, the mic desperately clutched in in one hand as if it's a talisman able to ward off this evil onslaught.

'It's now my turn,' Aliya says. She is surprised at the hardness in her voice.

She yanks the mic from Zin Yee and selects her song. The music plays. The lyrics appear over a scene of gondolas plying Venice's murky canals.

Aliya wriggles her bottom and begins to sing. The air rising powerfully and well-controlled from her abdomen up her lungs and through her vocal cords. A well-refined instrument.

Ohh . . . my voice is truly marvellous!

Its angelic quality fills the room. It echoes and soars, swirls in its sensuousness. Yes, it's the voice of a super diva. The TV flickers and there he is on screen.

Air . . . handsome face glowing, grinning encouragingly at her as the lyrics slip to the bottom of the screen.

'You're amazing, Aliya!' Air exclaims when she finishes the song. 'Pick another one.'

Aliya does so. 'Oh, I'm so glad you're here. Look, can you see what I did? Can you see they're all dead?'

'Yes, well done. They had to die. I'm so proud of you.'

Music plays, the lyrics now streams beside Air's handsome face. Her voice rises like wind through snowy mountains, like a breeze across jungle rivers, floating from a most wondrous musical instrument made in heaven.

'Oh, I love this song, Aliya. Your singing makes it even more special. So, so incredible. So amazing. You're going to be a great star!'

There's a knock on the door. Someone trying to get in. The doorknob turns. But it's locked. Aliya wonders what they'll think when they eventually see the dead bodies. It turns urgently. Then stops.

Ram is curled on the carpet beside the door like an embryo. The first to collapse, he muttered that he needed the toilet then turned to stare at them as his mouth foamed. He dropped to his knees, his mouth opening and closing as if he was singing before his eyeballs swam in their sockets.

Aliya glances around. Zin Yee is curled in a corner, tongue lolling out of her mouth. How silly she looks. Where is all that prettiness now?

No more lols for you!

Aliya almost laughs but manages to keep singing.

Poor Kai is slumped on the sofa, head bent as if he's contemplating the secret world within his groin. Handsome, funny Kai but now so very dead. SK is perched on the sofa, head slumped on the table beside those lethal half-emptied jugs of beer. She realizes that he's balding.

But he'll bald no more!

Now she does laugh. It's loud and merry. She has never laughed so hard in her life.

'Yes! yes!' Air cries. 'Singing is joyful. We can sing and laugh and be so very happy. Keep singing. Let your voice rise up proud! Oh, we must do a duet, you and I. How about this one?'

The music changes to one of the latest hits. It's a duet that she loves.

So together they sing, Air and Aliya. Her voice is even more glorious now and Air's voice is deep, soulful, resonating with mysterious power. Their voices mix and meld together, the whole so much better than their separate parts.

'Oh, fantastic,' declares Air when the song ends. 'I always knew you were the one. Our voices are so perfect as one. We will sing duets together for always.'

Aliya nods eagerly.

'You sing like an angel,' Air continues. 'You know why? Because you are now an angel, my angel.'

'You sing like an angel too,' Aliya says.

Air grins. 'That's because I am one.'

Suddenly, he is no longer on the screen. For he is right there, standing beside her, a cheeky (*devilish?*) smile on his face. A face that's glowing with dark intense eyes brimming with secrets. He's much taller than her and wears a shiny black robe that falls to the floor. Aliya can't believe it.

How can he just appear like that? Like magic?

He takes her hand. Caresses it. His skin is so soft and smooth but his touch is so, so cold. But she doesn't mind. Because she can sing!

'Y-You're an angel?'

Air nods. 'Yes, I am. A fallen angel. One of several. And I have many names. But, oh, I've been so lonely. I've been singing my songs alone for longer than I can remember. But now I have you and we can sing duets forever. Into an everlasting eternity!'

Aliya frowns. 'So no recording contracts?'

'No, we don't need those. Recording contracts give you nothing but gold and fame, which, in the end, you'll despise. You'll just end up a diva, pumped up with drugs and alcohol, drowning yourself in a hotel bathtub. Or you'll just get hideously old and plastic surgery is just going to turn you into an awful freak. No, you don't want that either.

'But I'll give you immortality. Everlasting life. Our singing will bring mankind ceaseless craving and drunken desire. Make them mistake love from lust. Sorrow from hate. Our songs will whisper in their dreams, and even while awake we can slip in between their thoughts.'

'What about womenkind?'

'Yes, we'll do that too. Angels don't need to use gender-neutral language, my dear. You understand that, don't you? But I'll say "humankind" if that makes you happier. And I only want you to be happy. For we'll be together for always. Lovers singing through eternity.'

He reaches with his other hand and takes hers. Holding both her hands, her bends over and puts his cold lips on hers.

'Let us sing, Aliya!'

Together they croon some older hits, then boomer songs from decades past, then pre-war show tunes and so like ghosts they slip back in time. Aliya is surprised that she knows the music, the lyrics, in all languages, so well. They sing centuries-old folk and traditional songs and funeral dirges, followed by ancient religious chants from naked dancing figures carrying flaming torches at bloody human sacrifices.

Air grins at her gleefully, dark shadows rising like a malevolent sea all around him. His eyes hollowed out by inky blackness. 'Oh, we sing so wonderfully together. Now say you want to be with me. Forever!'

Aliya nods eagerly. 'I . . . I want to be with you . . . *forever.*'

Air chortles, his teeth sharp, his voice echoing from a coffin. 'Then it is done! Mankind . . . *humankind* cannot resist!'

The room trembles and shimmers. The four bodies like dead dogs are but vague shadows. Or memories long gone. Just like the life she once lived.

'You are mine, Aliya. I am yours. In this honeymoon of ours we will sing the praises to Satan. The greatest fallen angel of them all! We will be his undying chorus!'

Blackness swamps them. Red flames rise all around.

Instead of burning heat, it's freezing cold.

Air is floating now, rising high. He is splendidly naked, his hairless body taut with muscles, bony white skin glowing, arms stretching out, fingers like worms wriggling in celebration. 'Sing, Aliya. Sing!'

The room is gone. In its place is what looks like a black cathedral or a gigantic cave or an endless shadowed dwelling for fallen angels. She doesn't even mind the rotting stench or the smell of burning bodies.

For she can sing!

Her body, so very cold but wonderfully naked, rises as her voice soars up to join his.

Air grabs hold of both her hands and, joyfully laughing, they spin like a whirlwind into the pungent darkness.

Can you hear them singing?

The Festival

I stared at my phone, not believing my eyes.

A Dog Eating Festival?

No way.

But there it was, in black and white, on social media.

Dog Eating Festival—Come Enjoy a Yummylicious Day!

Not only was the festival being held this Saturday, it was going to be at a park just a couple of blocks from where I lived. It was where teenagers played football on some evenings and where the oldies practised Tai Chi in the mornings.

As a Malay and a Muslim, we were supposed to stay away from dogs but I still couldn't believe people wanted to eat these lovely creatures. Yes, that's right I used the word *lovely*.

That's because I do like dogs. Actually I *love* them.

No, Fatehah, you can't love them. They're unclean. Muslims can't touch them.

That's what my mum said when I was a child and wanted to go pat those cute pooches I saw wandering on leashes near the shops, especially those adorable poodles. Of course, owning a dog was out of the question no matter how I begged.

As I got older, I looked into why Muslims couldn't touch dogs.

'That's because we follow the Shafi'i school, mum,' I protested. 'Other Muslim traditions allow us to keep dogs as pets.'

'Well, we're not having one,' mum said.

'Not even a cute little puppy?' I pleaded. 'I promise to look after it. I'm already fifteen and will be fully responsible. I'll wash myself properly seven times too with soil and water after touching it.'

'No, my decision's final,' mum said. 'What will our friends and relatives think if we have a dog? Anyway, we live in a condo and they don't allow dogs.'

'But some of our neighbours have dogs, mum. I see them all the time. This is a pet-friendly condo.' But I knew this was a losing battle. Religion trumped condo byelaws any time.

Mum shook her head dismissively and wandered back into the kitchen.

On my twenty-first birthday, a couple of months ago, I asked my father if I could have a puppy.

'Go ask your mother,' he said and wearily sipped his coffee.

He didn't want to get into an argument.

I'd been hounding my parents about getting a puppy since I was a kid and, although I was the only child and somewhat spoilt I'll admit, they flatly refused my request.

I once asked my father: 'Religion should be about doing good deeds right?'

'Of course. Islam brings light to this world. The light of Allah.'

'But then why have silly laws with no real meaning? Why say cute little puppies are foul creatures? Why say we can't play with pooches?'

'Don't talk anymore about this,' he snapped. 'Don't criticize our religion. If you need answers you can ask the *ustaz*. If you question our religion, you'll get into big trouble, understand? You remember that guy who had a dog-patting festival for Muslims? He got so many death threats? You want to be like him?'

I shook my head. 'But . . . but is it okay to become a vet, *abah*. I think that's what I'd really like to do.'

He glared at me. 'So that you can play with dogs? You might even have to work with pigs. You want that?'

That brought an end to the conversation. But it didn't stop my dreams of wanting to heal dogs and animals.

Not having a pooch of my own, I instead stared adoringly at photos and videos of these cute furry friends on social media and I spent as much time as possible with friends who had dogs.

I turned back to my phone.

Dog Eating Festival.

Horrible.

* * *

The next day, I met Yvonne, Siew Kong and Thevan at our usual hang out: a café inside a link house. We were all friends from secondary school but were now at different colleges doing our various degrees or diplomas.

The café owner allowed Yvonne and Siew Kong to bring their pooches as long as we leashed them at a tree beside the entrance. Sipping our coffees outside, the Poodle and German Shepherd were even given biscuits and a bowl of drinking water.

When we met this time, our conversation quickly turned to the disgusting dog eating festival.

'It's awful,' said Yvonne. 'How can they promote eating dogs?'

'Yeah,' added Siew Kong. 'Surely there must be a law against this. It must be illegal. And it's so cruel, don't you think?'

Thevan shook his head. 'But why do you think it's so cruel? It's no different from eating cows and chickens.'

We all knew that Thevan didn't like dogs. He was bitten as a child and so suffered from dog phobia; or *cynophobia* he would say, keen as he was to tell us its proper name.

'Ah come on, Thevan,' Yvonne said. 'Pooches are intelligent and so cute too. They're so different from cows and chickens.'

Thevan, who was tall and skinny, smiled at her. I had long worked out that Yvonne, with her fair skin and mischievous eyes, was the reason he always joined us, despite the two dogs hanging around which made him extremely nervous.

'Who says cows and chickens are less intelligent than dogs?' he replied. 'I think they're very intelligent. And sure, they're not as cute as dogs, but eating them is cruel too.'

'We've been eating chickens and cows all our lives,' Yvonne protested.

I doubted that she knew that Thevan liked her romantically. Yvonne's mind flitted from subject to subject like a little bird.

'But dogs are our pets,' Siew Kong added. 'We can't eat them.'

Thevan nodded. 'I once had a chicken as a pet. When my mum slaughtered it, I couldn't eat it.'

'So you see what I mean then,' Siew Kong said.

'But I could eat *other* chickens,' Thevan countered. 'Because they weren't my pets. So it's the same with dogs. If the dog isn't your pet, then you should have no problem eating it.'

Yvonne frowned. 'You can't be serious. You mean you *want* to eat dogs?'

'You know I don't. I'm just trying to point out that there isn't much difference between cows, pigs, chickens and dogs. Anyway, I'm a Hindu so I can't eat cows. But I'm not sure about dogs.'

'Well, we must all go to this dog eating festival and protest!' Siew Kong declared. 'I'm surprised the authorities are allowing such an awful thing.'

'Maybe they don't even know,' I said. 'That's why there's hardly any notice. It's going to be in three days. Hope you guys are free.'

'Hey, but maybe this is just someone's big joke,' said Yvonne. 'We'll go there to protest and there won't even be a festival.'

Siew Kong shook his head. 'Well, if it's a joke, it's really stupid. It's no laughing matter. Who wants to eat such beautiful creatures.

I'm going to bring Dim Sum. How could anyone think of eating my beautiful Poodle.'

* * *

So they all turned up that early Saturday morning beside my condo.

We strolled for a couple of blocks to the park. It was a cloudy day and wasn't too hot. A light breeze rippled against my headscarf.

I held onto Yvonne's arm as Manja, her German Shepherd, trotted eagerly beside her, straining on its leash. Siew Kong strolled up ahead wearing a loose Vans T-shirt which hid his extra kilos. Dim Sum, his brown Poodle, had stopped at a tree to urinate.

'Why do dogs have more rights than humans?' Thevan quipped. 'Why can't I go around pissing and shitting wherever I like in public?'

I giggled. 'That's because you're not as cute as a pooch, Thevan!'

'So if I wore a cute mask, then I can?'

Yvonne laughed. 'You're so silly, Thevan. You'll get arrested.'

The park was surrounded by a chain-link fence. We entered through a small gate at one corner of the football pitch, behind a football goal post.

As we strolled across the grass, my body stiffened.

A large red marquee stood in the centre of the playing field. The other goal post stood at the far end, partially blocked by the red tent. A colourful children's playground stood at one side of the football pitch.

We headed towards a small crowd who had gathered in front of the marquee.

A rock and roll number from hidden speakers spilled over us.

I couldn't believe it.

It was really happening!

I turned to Yvonne. 'Are these people here to eat dog meat?'

'I don't think so, Fatehah,' she said, as we got closer. 'They've all brought their pooches with them.'

To my delight, I realized that everyone had dogs on leashes.

'Maybe they want to get their dogs cooked?' Thevan said, grinning widely, his white teeth flashing. 'Roasted, stewed, sushi and sashimi.'

'Don't be silly, you,' Yvonne said. 'They've come to protest. Like us!'

'Looks like it,' Siew Kong added as he tried to control Dim Sum who was jumping around excitedly. 'See the placards.'

As we got closer we could hear the chanting.

Siew Kong gestured to a corner of the marquee. 'Let's go around the side. We can make our way to the front and see what's really happening.'

We followed him down one side of the marquee, and then made our way towards the front of the crowd.

Elvis Presley's 'Hound Dog' blared from a speaker.

I turned to Thevan. 'Can you smell it?'

'Yeah, dog meat being cooked.'

'It's disgusting,' I snorted.

He shrugged. 'Well, you only think that because dogs are cute. You know millions of dogs are eaten every year. In Korea, India, Vietnam . . .'

I wanted to tell him to shut up but Yvonne pulled my arm.

'Look,' she said, pointing inside the tent. 'They're cooking dog meat!'

Two chubby women and a long-haired man stood behind a couple of BBQ grilles and a long table draped with a red tablecloth. The women, who looked like twins, had short hair, dyed light brown, held metal spatulas and swayed horribly to the rock and roll beat.

The man stood his back to us, his muscular body unmoving, rock-like. A circular tattoo covered half his back.

The depiction of a blue lake, a stand of fir trees and a snowy mountain was breathtaking. I'd never seen anything like it. Muslims aren't allowed tattoos and I thought them ugly, but, despite my disgust over what they were cooking, this gorgeous tattoo changed my mind.

On the grilles, sizzling, spitting and smoky, were two long row of satay sticks.

My stomach squirmed.

A large red banner proclaimed: *Dog Eating Festival—It's going to be a Yummylicious Day!*

No, it damn well wasn't!

We were going to stop it. I didn't see how this dumb festival could continue with this crowd of twenty or more people chanting and shouting slogans in front of the marquee. I guessed that there were an equal number of furry friends on leashes, made up of dog breeds of all kinds. A few of them were rolling happily on the grass and I even saw a stray mongrel dog giving itself a good scratch. How were they to know that their own kind was being cooked just several feet away?

A stupid song about a dog named Boo now blared. The two women in the Marquee seemed to like this one as they were shaking their shoulders and big breasts to it, wide grins on their chubby faces.

'No dog eating! No dog eating!' A Chinese aunty in a green dress bellowed. I couldn't agree more. Her English Mastiff, quite unaware of its kind being cooked, sat indolently beside her, head inquisitively cocked.

An Indian uncle shook his placard, his white beard trembling as he chanted while his two Chihuahuas excitedly yapped from a baby pram. A white middle-aged man in a hat, his young son and daughter seemingly trying to hide behind him, pumped a fist in the air, while his black Labrador stretched on the grass, its rear paw blissfully scratching its ear.

Leashed to a chubby young man, a medium-sized dog, whose breed I couldn't identify was barking and a Beagle beside a white-haired elderly aunty was whining. Perhaps the pooches were trying to join in the protesting chant.

And so they should!

Despite the awful reason for gathering, I couldn't help grinning as I admired these lovely dogs all gathered in one spot. I so wished my parents would allow me to have one. Perhaps one day when I moved from home.

But would my husband, if I ever got married, allow me a dog? Maybe that would be my criteria for a husband.

No pet pooch, then no marriage!

'Look!' Siew Kong said, pointing angrily.

Following his finger across the playing field, I saw two men and two women strolling towards the marquee. To my horror, I realized that they didn't bring along any dogs and instead carried picnic mats and tiffin carriers. As they got closer, they stopped, glanced at each other, turned and fled.

'Bloody dog eaters!' Yvonne growled. 'We chased them away.'

'Serves them bloody right,' I said. 'How can anyone want to eat dogs?'

Thevan shrugged. 'Well millions do. Would you rather they starved?'

'Well, I'm sure they can eat other things,' I hissed.

I was getting quite fed up of him and his preaching.

In the marquee, the two plump twins, waving spatulas, glanced at the crowd and grinned at each other as if sharing a secret. Their red aprons read the same awful message:

Dog Eating Festival—It's going to be a Yummylicous Day!

The tall, dark man with that stunning tattoo still had his back to us. Then he turned towards me and, though I hated what he was doing, I couldn't help staring at his muscular body. Grey-hair falling across his shoulders, his eyes were intense, brimming with energy filled with secrets. Secrets dark and ancient. Even though deep wrinkles lined his face like undulating map contours, he exuded a youthful vigour.

He grinned at me. 'Welcome, welcome, friends! Welcome to our festival! What can I do for the four of you? I see you're keen to be at the front of the crowd. Would you like some satay or a kebab perhaps?'

A large hunk of meat rotated vertically on a metal skewer behind him, dripping with grease. The meaty stench was nauseating.

I sneered and turned away from him, so did the others.

'Awful!' Yvonne sneered. 'How can they be serving dog meat?'

'Well, no one's going to eat it,' I hissed.

'Yep,' added Thevan. 'I don't see any dog eaters here. They're all dog lovers. People who spend their time picking up dog shit. Dog-shit pickers. This is what human civilization has come to. Sad and degrading.'

'Dogs are wonderful!' Siew Kong snapped. 'They're our companions!'

Thevan glared back. 'Well, why don't you find some human ones instead. Or perhaps adopt a starving child? Billions of dollars are wasted on dog food while millions of people starve. You don't see how sickening that is?'

I didn't bother answering him and turned away. Siew Kong did the same and we both glanced back at the marquee.

The long-haired man loudly clapped his hands.

Once. Twice. Thrice.

The crowd stopped chanting and stared.

He stepped forward and placed his hands on the red tablecloth. The crowd looked so furious that if it wasn't for the long table serving as a a barrier, I was sure they would pounce on him and his two helpers.

'Welcome all of you!' he cried, his large mouth grinning. 'We've got mouth-watering kebabs and satay. No need to protest. I see some of you are not so happy with this exciting festival.'

'This is a bloody disgrace,' yelled the white-bearded Indian uncle as he waved his placard. His other hand pushed his Chihuahuas in the pram forward as if he wanted to ram the table. 'No civilised people should be eating dogs. Shut it down now!'

'Oh, but you're got it all wrong, my friends. If you think this dog eating festival is for eating dogs, well you've got your French Bulldogs and Boston Terriers mixed up. I'm holding this dog eating festival because of my *love* for dogs!'

'Yes, we know that,' growled the Indian uncle. 'You love eating them. But nobody else does!'

'Oh, no, no, no . . . you misunderstand me, my friends. I'm cooking chicken and beef here. Not dog meat.'

I turned to Yvonne and frowned. She stared at me, confused. *What did he mean? He wasn't cooking dog meat?*

The man laughed and shook his head, his grey hair swishing about his broad shoulders. 'The chicken and beef are for you if you want it. It's delicious food but, for me, it's just part of our show. The real bait is this festival itself which you foolish dog owners have completely misunderstood.'

'What the hell do you mean?' the white guy demanded. He sounded German. His son and daughter stood hid behind him, looking on apprehensively.

The long-haired man bared his teeth to the crowd, teeth that seemed extraordinarily white and big, his voice getting more strident. 'You've been keeping your hounds as slaves for all these years. Imprisoning them in your homes. Forcing them to be your companions, when they should be outdoors scavenging, running wild and free in packs with only the wind in their faces.

'Do you know how many dogs are euthanized every year because owners no longer want to take care of them? Millions and millions. Euthanasia is just another word for murder.'

'That's got nothing to do with this stupid festival of yours!' cried the white-haired elderly aunty, raising her walking stick at him. Her Beagle was staring up at her, licking its lips.

'Oh, but it really does, my friend.'

'You don't call me that,' she hissed. 'You are certainly *not* my friend!'

'Oh, but I disagree. Aren't dogs man's best friend?'

She waved her walking stick at him again. 'I don't know what you're talking about.'

'Maybe you do, maybe you don't. But all of you dog owners have got it completely wrong. As I said, this dog eating festival is not about eating dog meat. It's for dogs who no longer want to be your prisoners. It's for dogs who want to be free from that prison you call home, where all they can hope for is being taken for some lousy walk occasionally. It's for dogs who yearn for revenge. And, by that, I mean *all* of them!'

He turned to the chubby twins and whispered.

They nodded and licked their lips.

Then he placed one foot on the table and kicked it over.

The twins hauled themselves over the fallen table, their fleshy bodies quivering.

As they approached the protesters, their ears and noses began to wriggle. Their faces started to contort. Their noses and ears, quite impossibly, grew longer. The shape of their heads elongated. This was crazy for now white fur sprouted from their faces. They raised their distorted heads and loudly moaned as if in both hunger and pain, then, with a single cry, fell on all fours to the grass.

'Shit . . .' blurted the Indian uncle. 'I don't bloody believe it!'

'What the hell?' cried the white guy. 'Madness!'

The protesters retreated, faces ashen, dragging their pooches away.

We backed away too. I couldn't believe my eyes. My heart was thumping so hard.

Then the twins, who were surely no longer women, turned their heads upwards and howled, like . . . like *dogs!*

Yvonne glanced wide-eyed at me, her pale face so stricken I could barely recognized her.

'What the hell's happened to them!' Thevan cried, pulling her away. 'This is insane!'

I could hardly breathe. Everything seemed to go out of focus.

Then the dogs, from the Chihuahua to the Mastiff, were howling too. Manja, Yvonne's German Shepherd, sat on the grass and bayed so loudly that I had to put my hands to my ears.

'Be quiet, Manja,' Yvonne yelled. 'Be quiet!'

But her commands were drowned by the mad howling.

Then I realized that the howling twins had disappeared and in their place stood two white fluffy Chow Chows. Suddenly, these hounds stopped their baying and glared at the protesters, teeth bared, saliva dripping.

I couldn't believe my eyes. This had to be a nightmare and I was still tucked safely in bed. But no, it was too real. Here I was seeing the crowd retreat, babbling and knocking into each other and getting their dog leashes tangled.

'What . . . what's going on here?' shrieked the elderly aunty. 'This . . . this can't be real!'

'Where the hell did those two dogs come from?' someone bellowed, panic in his voice.

It was a stupid question for we knew the answer. We had witnessed their impossible transformation.

Then the long-haired man, leapt over the table, legs splayed on the grass, naked chest glistening and raised his muscular arms in the air. His dark throat trembled and he . . .

Barked!

It was a command for suddenly one of the Chow Chows leapt forward and sank its teeth into the elderly aunty's thigh. She screamed, dropped her walking stick, and fell to the grass, legs kicking out. Instead of defending her mistress, her Beagle, whom she must have loved and pampered for years, growled and rushed to her throat.

The other Chow Chow lunged at the white man's calf. He yelled and tried to hit it but his own hound had turned on him and sunk its teeth into his pale thigh, ripping out bloody flesh. He screamed and fell forwards, his hat tumbling away like a frisbee.

The green-dressed aunty now faced cold betrayal, for her Mastiff leapt and knocked her over. It stood over its owner, growling, saliva dripping from its barred teeth, eyes filled with hate. Then it lunged. She shrieked as blood sprayed.

Placards were falling.

Dogs were attacking.

Their bewildered owners screamed in surprise and flesh-tearing pain, most dragged like hunks of meat to the grass, now slicked red. From the speaker, a merry song blared over the bloody carnage.

About a doggy in the window. And the price to be paid.

'Feast, feast, my children!' cried the long-haired man in a delirious rapture. 'Take your revenge and eat your meat. This dog eating festival is just for you. Eat as much as you like. Enjoy the human flesh!'

All around were snarling, leaping, rabid dogs, their owners pathetically trying to fight them off. The pram lay on its side, one wheel spinning in the air as the Chihuahua tried to bite off the Indian uncle's fingers while the other gnawed his ear.

The white guy's daughter wailed, one arm half ripped off. The son's belly was a bloody mess, his hands raised protectively against a big, red-eyed hound.

I turned away from the mad massacre that spun about me, back to the red marquee. The long-haired man was gone.

Instead, there stood a big dog. I blinked. No, this was no dog. It was a huge white-furry . . .

Wolf!

I gasped as in a single bound it flew at the protesters, snarling and biting, left and right, blood spraying in fountains. Then lunging, going for the kill.

To my horror, I saw Yvonne unmoving on the ground, her blouse soaked in blood. Manja stared at me, its mouth dribbling, its teeth dripped red.

Thevan knelt beside her, sobbing. Her throat had been ripped out.

Siew Kong was limping away, Dim Sum, snapping at his heels.

Then the Mastiff, in a single leap, brought him down. The big dog was at this throat.

Dim Sum, no cute dog now, lunged at his groin, then snapped its head back, its mouth blood-filled and bits of flesh hung from its teeth. Then a pale ripped-out testicle, like a hairy ping-pong ball, rolled out before being snapped up again and eagerly swallowed.

I wanted to rush over even though there wasn't much I could do but there, blocking my path, stood the huge wolf. Its white fur bright, bristling and . . .

Beautiful!

I couldn't help realizing what a gorgeously magnificent animal it was even though my life was in danger.

Its bulging muscles quivered with raw power. Its sharp teeth gleamed and dripped blood. Its fierce intelligent eyes, filled with dark secrets, burned into mine.

What was it saying?

Was it that wolves were the ancient ancestors of all dogs from the smallest Chihuahua to the biggest Mastiff, that from its DNA sprouted every hound from the purest prized breeds to the mixed-up mutts that scavenged the streets?

I shook my head and blinked.

Where did that strange thought come from?

The wolf took a slow, graceful step forward.

It strongly smelt of zoos.

Blood pulsed in my head. My throat dry.

Was it going to attack? Was I going to die?

I stood there, paralyzed by its unflinching stare, unable to move.

Then someone grabbed my arm.

'Let's get out of here!' Thevan cried.

He pulled me away and then we were stumbling past bloody bodies, past moaning, dying people, snarling and biting dogs, and we were running across the grass.

I glimpsed a man trying to climb the chain-link fence, but a dog had its teeth in his leg and was dragging him to the ground. A grey dog was bounding across the grass to join the attack. There was nothing I could do.

We fled past the football goal post and then we were through the gate.

Once on the street, we ran until we got to the main road.

'Why didn't they attack us?' I asked, breathing hard, my hair wet beneath my headscarf.

'Don't know,' Thevan said, sweat dripping down his scared, bewildered face. 'Maybe . . .' he panted hard . . . 'it's because we're not dog owners.'

I stared, hardly believing him.

It had to be true.

Hands trembling, Thevan pulled out his phone, almost dropping it on the road. 'I have to call an ambulance.'

I nodded and slid mine out. 'I'll call the police. They have to catch all those dogs. Maybe they have rabies or something.'

But I didn't believe my own words.

That man . . . he had done something.

Some strange dark magic. But he was no man.

He was a wolf!

I shuddered. Then my whole body shivered.

Before I could make the call, I was kneeling on the pavement, vomiting.

Then I passed out.

* * *

The police, when they finally arrived, found not a single dog. The hounds had vanished. The ambulance men couldn't do much for the bloodied bodies, the protesters who had their throats or bellies ripped out, stomachs and intestines eaten away. As for the red marquee and the cooked meat within, there was no trace.

My parents didn't believe me when I told them about the carnage. I just lay weeping in bed, earphones jammed in, trying to lose myself. Trying to forget what had happened.

But I managed to drag myself to Siew Kong and Yvonne's funerals. Thevan and I stared at each other but we couldn't find the words to say to make sense of what happened. Maybe we were trying to forget about it or to somehow make sense of it. Perhaps we were both still in shock.

I felt cold and numb inside. It was as though I'd be broken up and pieced together so badly that I no longer recognized myself.

The nightmares did eventually stop but sometimes the white wolf still approached in the fitful shadows of my dreams, the marquee fluttering like a flag in the misty distance. Or sometimes he emerged from a stand of fir trees, a snowy mountain in the distance, padding its way to me beside the shores of a crystal blue lake and licking my hand.

It was strangely comforting. It felt as though there was some meaning to all of it.

Just months later, I got the news that the scholarship I had applied for was approved. I was going to study Veterinary Medicine in the UK. To my surprise, my parents didn't object and I assured them that I wouldn't be working on dogs or pigs.

So off I went the following year, living in another country and meeting people from so many other nations. Because of the cooler weather, people enjoyed strolling outdoors at all times of the day, many with pooches. But winters were freezing and often drizzling all day. People still ventured out though and I would stop to pat their furry companions.

It made me smile and brought a warmth to my heart.

But after news came that Thevan had died in a motorbike accident, I became less inclined to do so. He had said some things that I disagreed with but now began to find disturbingly true.

After graduating, I worked as a vet. I messaged my parents that I didn't treat any dogs as I worked exclusively with horses, although this was a lie. When I returned to Malaysia for my father's sixtieth birthday, I did admit to treating pooches.

'You're in England,' he said. 'You can do what you want. Nobody here knows or really cares what you're doing over there. Just don't work with dogs when you come back to Malaysia, okay?'

'Of course,' I said, nodding eagerly. 'It wouldn't be right.'

I was thankful for his understanding. As I was out of the country, I was beyond the reach of those who's life's mission was to judge others. Perhaps he also knew that I was now a salaried professional and no longer in his control.

I never returned to Malaysia for I married an English school teacher and we moved to a cottage in a quiet village beside a forest. Our home was near one of many walking tracks. I was often tempted to keep a pooch and this would have been a perfect place.

Except I didn't.

For I always remembered the wolf.

For he still sometimes visits in dreams, creeping through the forest undergrowth and licking my fingers or bounding towards me and, on the shores of that cold blue lake. I would hold his furry white neck and kiss his nose.

Once it had whispered:

Pet dogs are no better than pampered prisoners. Don't fool yourself into thinking that their submissive behaviour is happiness.

Find joy without them . . .

My husband had told me he would like a pooch but I smiled sadly and said no. I never told him about the dog eating festival for he would think me mad. But I did tell him about the white wolf in my dreams and I like to think he understood the message.

We often ramble along the forest tracks, just the two of us, saying hello to fellow walkers and their assortment of dogs, but mostly enjoying our own company and our simple life.

As for that Dog Eating Festival, I can hardly believe it happened. With Thevan gone, I'm its only witness and I'll keep it a secret, a dark secret that I will take to my grave.

Moongate

The sun had barely risen when I parked the car.

'Got everything?' Anna asked as we slid out.

I nodded.

We both wore face masks. Masks had become an intrinsic part of our lives in these COVID days. I longed for a time when I never had to wear them again.

We stepped through the Moongate, a circular walled entrance that marked the beginning of the walking track. It was once an entrance to a Chinese tycoon's 19th-century mansion but the building was long gone.

After we had our temperatures checked and registered, we took off our masks, which I gladly did, and I wondered if it would ever end for infections still soared and new virus variants kept emerging. And if COVID was eventually defeated, what other more lethal viruses were waiting for us?

Anna strode on ahead up the wending track into the embrace of trees and insect shrills. I took a moment to breathe the cool, fresh air, filled with jungle scents and felt my senses tingling with life.

I followed her up a series of earthen steps held together by short concrete risers. Tree roots, some as thin as cords, others as thick as sleeping pythons meandered along the track. Tree trunks, of various girths, rose to a canopy dappled in sunlight.

I took joy in this, being out in nature, where, in truth, we all belonged.

Anna stopped to snap a photo of a pitcher plant growing on a tree trunk. Next she videoed a trail of black ants that meandered like a conquering army over the clay soil.

She tapped my shoulder to point at several monkeys frolicking in the trees.

One gave me a hard stare with big unblinking eyes.

Then it hissed, teeth clenched, long and loud, before scampering away.

Anna laughed. 'Don't think it liked you.'

I didn't think it was funny. 'Not sure why it did that,' I said, frowning.

It strangely felt like a warning.

I shrugged and we carried on climbing the steps, past several boulders, some smooth and jagged, others incredibly huge and covered in lichen.

Up ahead, through entangling vines, I glimpsed a patch of yellow and wondered what it was. Then, turning a corner, I saw her . . . a woman in a yellow dress.

A *cheongsam.*

As we approached, I saw that she clutched a brown paper umbrella that slowly swayed like a rain cloud beneath the foliage.

Gazing at her lovely clothes, I felt most odd. Why would she wear those on this humid jungle trail?

Now just a few feet from her, I noticed that her hair was tied in a bun and its gold decorative hair clip glittered in the dappled sunlight. A small red handbag was strapped across her body and she slowly strolled, almost in slow motion, yellow shoes barely touching the ground.

As we overtook the woman, a sweet fragrance hit me. An expensive musky perfume that didn't belong on this jungle-trail.

I glimpsed her delicate smooth hands too and a dark stain on the umbrella with a small tear like a teardrop just above it.

Striding on past her, I stole a backwards glance.

She was young, perhaps in her twenties, thin-faced and pale, wearing bright red lipstick. Her eyes though were closed which struck me as utterly weird.

When she was out of sight, I turned to Anna.

'Did you see her?'

She frowned. 'You mean that woman with the cheongsam?'

I nodded. 'Yeah, she was . . . so *off.*'

'Surely you don't mean *off*, you mean *odd*, don't you?'

'I don't know, she was just like, I don't know, like a . . . *ghost.*'

'A ghost? You're kidding? She was strange that's all, with that cheongsam and those heeled shoes!'

'But she was walking with her eyes closed.'

Anna grinned. 'Maybe she was doing a walking meditation!'

Normally I would laugh, instead I just shrugged.

We had reached the bottom of a set of steep steps known as Jalan Chuan. It was the most arduous part of our hike.

Anna slapped my back. 'Let's go.'

Focusing on one step at a time, I ascended. It didn't take long for me to be breathing hard, wiping copious amounts of sweat from my brow. Anna, being much fitter, was well up ahead. She waited several times for me to catch up.

'You should stop smoking,' she said.

'I know. I'll try again. Maybe next month'

'And you should lose a bit of weight too.'

I chuckled. 'Perhaps I should try intermittent fasting.'

'Good idea. Everyone seems to be doing it.'

But what I wanted most was a smoke.

Except I didn't want to do it while hiking. It just didn't look good. Anyway I had been trying to stop too, ever since my elder brother died of COVID the year before. He was a chain-smoker and struggled with his weight. I needed to lose those kilos too.

Anna bent over to take photos of some tiny flowers.

I glanced up at the sunlight shimmering in the foliage above and wondered when it would end. Millions dead from the pandemic. A more deadly variant could bring on human extinction on this fragile planet. Maybe it wouldn't be such a bad thing seeing as how we were wrecking it.

I climbed the few remaining steps and reached the top. Anna followed behind as the track widened and straightened.

Then up ahead, through the trees, I spied a yellow glimmer and frowned. I turned the corner and saw the back of another woman.

In a yellow cheongsam.

She too held a paper umbrella.

I swallowed.

This wasn't another woman . . . it was the same person.

Had to be! But why did I think that?

Perhaps because she walked in that same slow motion, in that awful gliding way. Like a pallbearer in a jungle funeral.

But I told myself that it couldn't be the same woman, for we had left the other one well behind us.

As I neared the figure, who seemed hardly to be moving, a coldness tightened my stomach. She had that same gold hair clip and handbag worn across the body. The same red handbag bouncing like bloody flesh against the hip.

I swallowed. I didn't want to think it, but even as I gazed at her slow, slow, steps, I knew it was true. She was some kind of spirit, a ghost treading the path in the jungle.

I turned to Anna and gestured at the yellow figure.

Anna stared questioningly at me.

Did she think I was still being foolish? Or could she now see that the figure was not of this world?

We had almost reached the slow-walking figure which left me no choice.

As I hurried past, dragging Anna with me, I saw a dry, veined hand holding an umbrella. But that umbrella . . . it had that same dark stain with the same tear above it.

Shit!

And that same sweet smell too!

I could hardly breathe.

Striding on, I quickly glanced back . . . but no, it was not her. It was a much older, thin-faced woman, perhaps in her sixties, wearing the same red lipstick.

I didn't know if I was relieved or not and instead focused on placing one step in front of the other.

As we rounded a corner, Anna pulled her hand away.

'What's wrong?' I asked, frowning.

'You were holding my hand so tightly.'.

I shrugged while she massaged her fingers. 'Sorry, but did you see the woman?'

'Sure. But what about her?'

'It's . . . it's the same woman as before!'

Her mouth fell open. 'That's crazy. Just because they were both wearing a yellow cheongsam and carrying an umbrella. Don't know why they'd want to wear that while hiking and those heeled shoes, forget it!'

'But didn't you see their faces?' I said in a low voice.

She shook her head. 'Not really.'

'I tell you it was the same woman. But she had aged somehow. She had become a lot older. And she had her eyes closed too!'

She grabbed my arm. 'No way, you're imagining it!'

'No, I didn't. And the umbrella had the same dark stain and a rip above it.'

'Come on, don't get so worked up.'

'I'm not worked up.'

Then I grabbed her hand again and pulled her along with me.

I knew one thing though, I wasn't worked up.

I was *terrified*.

'Hey, why are you in such a hurry?'

'I . . . I just don't want to hang around.'

Anna gestured irritably toward a set of colourful steps. 'We're almost there anyway. That's Station Five.'

We climbed the steps which were painted in bright colours, up to Station Five which marked the end point of the walk where there was a rest area, public toilets and some old gym equipment. We would normally take a break here before heading back down.

But I didn't dare take a rest here or go back down.

The ghost would be approaching. If we stayed here, she would soon reach us, walking in that awful gliding way, umbrella in hand, handbag bouncing, eyes horribly closed.

I wondered if she had something to do with the tycoon's demolished house that was once fronted by the Moongate. I wanted to tell Anna this but she was immersed in her phone. Posting another photo on social media no doubt.

'Let's carry on,' I said.

'You want to walk on?'

I nodded.

'You never wanted to before. You always said it's too tiring.'

I tried to grin. 'Well, there's always a first time.'

I didn't want to mention the ghost.

'I'm feeling adventurous today.'

* * *

So we walked past Station Five.

The track was not as wide as before and foliage occasionally brushed our faces. As we pushed on, it became rougher and undulating and we had to sometimes duck under branches and scramble over rocks.

'Wow! Never seen these before.'

Anna had stopped to take photos of some red mushrooms.

'Are they poisonous?' I asked.

'Probably. So don't go eating them. I don't want to have to drag you to hospital. You're too heavy to carry.'

I bit my lip, dreading the idea of falling ill or getting injured on this lonely track.

'That wouldn't be good,' I muttered.

I scooted ahead, following the track that now sloped steeply upwards, passing a house-sized boulder that sat precariously above us. Further along, was a dead bird in the middle of the track. Flies buzzed over its yellow feathers. Ants swamped its open beak and maggots crawled out of its eyes.

I swallowed and stepped over it, half-expecting it to start flapping its dead wings. I glanced back just to make sure the thing was unmoving.

The track began to wind its way steeply downhill. It twisted and darkened as trees pressed in, the branches like claws that wanted to grab us and drag us screaming into the jungle.

Then, past a thicket of branches, I glimpsed it.

A patch of yellow.

My blood went cold.

No, no . . . this can't be.

I wanted to flee but I had to make sure.

As I turned the corner, I felt my legs go weak.

She wore the same yellow cheongsam. Her back to us, all hunched up. The paper umbrella.

Handbag strap across the body like a rotting carcass.

The slow walk of the dead.

Her hair, tied in a bun, had become a dirty white.

My heart was pounding.

I felt a hand on mine. I turned to see Anna's stricken face.

She knew something was wrong. She now realized that it wasn't my imagination.

'It's . . . her,' I whispered.

She nodded. 'But her hair's white.'

I glanced back at the figure.

My belly tightened. Sweat dripped down my forehead.

The woman had stopped. Still as a statue.

Her gold hair clip glittered ghoulishly.

What the hell does she want?

Was she waiting for us? Daring us to come forward?

Maybe she had a knife. She could stab us in a wild frenzy, leaving our bloodied corpses on this lonely track.

'W-We have to turn back,' I whispered.

At first I thought Anna would object, telling me that I was being foolish.

Instead she nodded, face pale.

She turned and led the way back, striding up the sloping track.

I quickly followed, glancing back several times, half expecting the ghost to come chasing after us, knife glinting. But thankfully, there was nothing but a desolate track, trees pressing in on both sides.

Once I caught a whiff of that sweet smell. Heart lurching, I glanced back and thought I glimpsed a shadow shifting within the trees. I stopped and stared. But saw nothing and hurried on.

As I stepped over the dead bird, flies swarmed upwards into my face. I gasped and brushed them off. I smelt something awful and hurried after Anna.

She was moving quickly and, breathing hard, I had a hard time catching up with her. The track descended steeply and suddenly Anna staggered and fell on one knee.

'Damn!' she cried. 'I've twisted my foot.'

'Is it okay?' I asked, quickly examining it. 'Can you walk?'

'I think it's all right. Just hurts a bit.'

'You need to be more careful. We don't have to rush. I don't think the woman's following.'

Anna nodded, but she still looked worried.

I took her hand and led her along at a slower pace.

Minutes later we were back at Station Five and I felt I could breathe again. Back to a civilization of sorts. We would surely be safe here amongst other people.

No one was around though except for an elderly couple sitting on a concrete bench beneath the shelter beside the public toilets. Three monkeys sat on a metal railing beside the cliff face that looked over the jungle below.

'I need to sit down,' Anna said, hobbling slightly. 'Have to rest my ankle.'

We sat on a bench away from the monkeys and I wiped the sweat off my brow.

I slowly turned to her. 'That woman. That was her again out there, wasn't it?'

Anna blinked. 'I think so. Even though her hair was all white.'

'But not a *her*, an *it*,' I whispered. 'A ghost.'

She frowned. 'Can't be. Maybe it's all just a coincidence. Sure three women, all wearing the same cheongsam and carrying a paper umbrella. Maybe it's just some kind of ritual.'

'You know that's not true. All three of them looked the same, they felt the same. And there was that same tear on the umbrella. Admit it, you were scared, weren't you?'

'Yes, yes, I was. There was something so *off* about that woman.'

She turned away, made a noise in her throat, and pulled out her phone.

The elderly couple got up. They strolled past and I watched them disappear.

* * *

I stared into the jungle below, listening to the insect shrills.

'I read about it online sometime back,' I said, almost to myself.

Anna frowned. 'What are you talking about?'

'The story of the yellow Beetle.'

'I prefer butterflies.'

'I'm not talking about an insect. It's the car, a yellow Volkswagen Beetle.'

'What about it?'

'One night two brothers were driving on the Karak highway. In front of them was this yellow Volkswagen Beetle going very slowly. So they had to overtake it but it was dangerous because the road was winding and hilly. But as they drove past, they saw that there was no one driving the car. It was empty!'

'That's bloody scary. But why are you suddenly telling me this?'

'Because after overtaking it, they saw the same car in front of them, going slowly and blocking the lane. So they had to overtake it again.'

'Hey, I've heard this story before. Didn't they make a movie out of it?'

'Yeah, maybe. Anyway, they overtook it again and, a minute later, there it was in front of them again. So they overtook it once more on that dangerous road. Many people have seen this yellow Volkswagen Beetle on that highway.'

'So you think . . .'

'Yes, I think this is something similar. It's not a yellow ghost car but a ghost wearing a yellow cheongsam.'

Then, through the trees, we heard music blaring. I turned to see a large boisterous group approaching, chatting loudly, and wielding walking sticks.

Anna frowned. 'Some people don't know how to respect this place. Come on, let's go.'

We got up, skirted past the group and headed back downhill but at a slower pace because of Anna's injured ankle. She continued to hobble but not as badly as before.

As we made our way down the steep steps, Anna holding my arm for support, a cool breeze swept over us. I shivered. Perhaps it was from the cold or maybe the shadows, like giant leeches from the undergrowth, that spilled like ink onto the track.

Mist fell upon us like giant grasping ghostly hands.

A drop of water struck my cheek. I glanced up at the canopy only to see a torrent descending. It splashed, first on my nose, followed by a cacophony like drums, all around us.

I grabbed Anna by the waist and pulled her along.

'We have to run,' I cried over the sound of the rain.

'No need,' Anna cried back over. 'We're already soaked!'

She was, of course, right. Mindful of her injured foot, we made our way as best as we could down the track which was now dangerously slippery. Because of the thick fog, we could only see several feet ahead. Streams of water ran rapidly downhill, each step a miniature waterfall.

Anna clutched my arm tightly. 'It's so cold and this fog is so creepy.'

'We'll get to the bottom soon. We have a towel in the car. We can dry up.'

'I don't want to get sick from this rain.'

'No, you won't. Come on, let's go.'

We reached the top of the long flight of steps and began our careful descent as rain lashed and wind howled against our faces.

We were half way down when I stopped.

'Fuck,' I whispered.

Anna had seen it too for her grip tightened on my arm, her nails biting into my skin.

Out of the fog, a solitary figure had emerged less than ten steps below.

It stood unmoving, like an ice statue, her hunched back to us. *No, this can't be happening!*

But there she was in that same yellow cheongsam. The handbag. The hair no longer in a bun. There were just strands of wiry white tangles that sprouted from a bare skull.

Rain splashed off the paper umbrella.

My stomach squirmed. I felt feverish, body cold and trembling.

What were we going to do? It was either flee back up the steps or overtake the ghost-woman and get back safely to our car.

'We just have to get past her,' I cried over the beating rain. 'Then we'll be fine.'

Anna turned to me, nodding, water like a flood of tears dripping down her cheeks.

In that one moment, I realized how beautiful she was and how much I loved her.

Whatever was going to happen would now happen. I couldn't stop it.

'I love you,' I said. 'So very much. Now let's do this.'

Then, grabbing her hand, we took the few steps towards the figure.

As we scurried past, my heart beating hard, I glimpsed the black stain on the umbrella, the rip above and a line of water streaming down it.

I grimaced, turning away, not wanting to set my eyes on the woman's face, and, keeping them glued on each step.

It was going to fine, we were going to . . .

Then Anna screamed.

I spun around and in a single terrible glance, not only saw Anna's horrified expression but the thing's face. For this was no woman.

For what should have been a face was a skull!

A pale grey skull where bits of flesh like leeches clung. The twin eye sockets were chasms of blackness that dragged me to madness.

Its skeleton hand lifted up the paper umbrella and the skull swivelled towards me, teeth rattling over the beating rain, mouth opening and closing like the restless lid of a coffin.

A high-pitched screech burst from it and lashed through the rain and trees.

I staggered back, lost my balance and fell backwards.

'Noooo!' I cried.

I was still holding Anna's hand and together we fell.

As we both tumbled down the steps, the skull grinned at us, before it vanished behind the fog.

* * *

Bright sunlight glimmered through the foliage.

My head throbbed. I smelled soil and rotting leaves.

There was a gathering of assorted shoes. I glanced up at the small crowd around me. Someone had placed a cloth beneath my head.

'We need to take him to hospital,' a voice said.

'Wait, wait, he's waking up,' came a woman's voice.

A bald old man knelt beside me. 'Maybe it wasn't such a bad fall.'

Concerned faces swam around me. Sound of water dripping. Rain had stopped. A whooping call came from far away. Noises echoed in my head.

'You fell down the steps,' the woman said. 'Good thing we found you. Are you okay?'

My head hurt. So did my right arm.

I slowly sat up and glanced at the walkers, huddled around me.

'Where's Anna?' I asked.

'Who's Anna?' a woman said. 'You were the only one here when we found you.'

'No, that can't be? She fell down the steps with me. After we saw that . . .'

That demon, I wanted to say.

But I didn't. No one would believe me.

I staggered to my feet.

'Maybe Anna's waiting in the car,' I mumbled.

But I realized that was a foolish thing to say as she would never leave me injured on the ground. But perhaps she went to get help. That had to be it.

But I didn't believe it. She had her phone and could easily have called for an ambulance. I slipped out my own device but there were no messages from her, no missed calls.

'You sure you'll be okay?' the woman asked.

'Yes, I'll be fine. Thank you. I have to go find her.'

So I followed the wet, winding, muddy track downhill, past other walkers coming in the opposite direction. I stopped several times along the way to call and message her but there was no response.

Where was she? And why wasn't she answering?

I glanced up at Moongate's circular entrance, sighed and stepped through it. I felt as though I was entering another world. One of cars and computers.

Standing at a loss on the pavement, I looked up and down the street at the wet bitumen, the parked cars, cyclists and enthusiastic walkers. Several had hiking sticks, some with masks, some without. A stray dog stared at me from across the road before turning away and scratching itself.

No sign of Anna. Where could she be? How could she just disappear like that?

I got into my car and dried myself with the towel that I always kept on the backseat. After taking a long swig from the water bottle, I lit a cigarette but my fingers trembled so much I could hardly light it. Then I called and messaged her several more times but it was useless.

She had simply vanished.

Not knowing what to do, I drove up to the Botanical Gardens but there was no sign of her. So I drove back past the Moongate, past the Hindu temples then turned back towards the gardens again.

Eventually I gave up and, feeling cold and exhausted, drove home to our condo.

The rest of that day was spent trying to contact her through her friends and relatives and even the hospitals. But Anna had simply disappeared.

That night, I lay awake in bed, my mind wracked with worry, going through every permutation. Where had she gone to?

The next day, my head spun so badly and I could hardly get out of bed. My forehead dripped with sweat and, at other times, I shivered as I wrapped myself tightly in my blanket.

Classic COVID symptoms?

No, it was surely my heart breaking.

'Where are you, Anna?' I whispered as I lay shivering on my soaked pillow. 'Where have you gone to?'

But at the back of my mind I knew what had happened. The demon had taken her, kidnapped her after we had fallen down the steps.

But taken her where?

A few days after Anna had vanished, I stared into the bathroom mirror and realized how haggard I looked. I hadn't shaved and my face was pale, my eyes haunted.

I collapsed on the living room sofa, staring out of the balcony, at the two plastic outdoor chairs, at the shopping mall being constructed across the highway, the cranes like hungry monsters.

I remembered us sitting on a bench at Station Five and I was telling her about the yellow Volkswagen Beetle. But there was more to the story.

The two brothers were petrified by what they saw. Their car had almost lost control as they overtook the Beetle but they managed to get back safely to KL.

They drove into the condo parking area and wound their way up the ramps to their designated parking spot, thinking about their close shave and the interesting story they could tell family and friends.

As the car made the turn past the lift lobby, there sitting in their designated parking spot was the yellow Beetle!

It had followed them home.

Suddenly, its reverse lights came on and the vehicle shot backwards with a screech and smashed into their car. The Beetle drove forward, then reversed again, ramming into their car, again and again.

The two men were later pulled out of the vehicle by security guards and taken to hospital. One brother died but the other one survived to tell the tale. As for the Beetle, it had disappeared.

Anna never got to hear the story's tragic ending.

Just thinking of the story exhausted me.

The sky had turned purple as daylight fled and the evening call to prayers moaned from loudspeakers, echoing from afar. I lay unmoving, watching the hues of the sky subtly change, until eventually darkness crept in.

Still I lay there lifeless, my heart devoid of feeling, my mind numb.

Then, another call to prayers and the full moon rose, spilling its eerie glow onto the outdoor chairs and onto the living room floor.

My hairs though now stood on end.

Hunched on one of the plastic chairs was a figure, its back to me.

A chill crawled slowly up my spine.

It clutched a closed paper umbrella in one hand.

Noooo!

Yellow cheongsam. Wiry white hair.

I could hardly breathe.

Sitting upright on the other chair was another silhouette.

Anna!

Wearing the same clothes as on our hike days ago.

She slowly stood up and her head turned towards me.

She had no eyes!

Just white sockets where the eyes should have been.

She reached a hand towards the seated figure. The demon took it, got up and the pale skull, sprouting wisps of white hair, swivelled towards me.

The black eye sockets met mine. Bits of flesh like leeches clung to the skull.

'Stay away from me,' I whispered. 'Please . . . no!'

The demon's teeth clattered as if saying something. It tapped the closed umbrella on the tiles and stepped, in a slow funeral-like motion, into the living room.

I smelt that sweet nauseating fragrance.

My body refused to move.

Before me, the skull glowed in the moonlight, bits of flesh dangling like worms. Anna leaned her head on the demon's shoulder, eyes sightless, lips curled in a death grin.

'We were waiting for the full moon,' she whispered. 'We only feast once a month.'

I shrieked as they lunged at me.

* * *

I opened my eyes.

The living room was bathed in moonlight.

My T-shirt covered in sweat.

Other than the noise of highway traffic and music from far away, I heard nothing else. No teeth clicking in a demonic skull or Anna whispering.

I glanced around.

Where was the loathsome demon? Where was the horrible thing that was once Anna? Was it just a nightmare?

I had wet myself. My shorts were soaked.

I pushed myself off the sofa and glanced about, my body cold and quivering, petrified that they could be hiding, crouched in the kitchen, slunk beneath the bed or standing behind the bathroom door.

Then I stumbled to the bathroom and had a long hot shower, praying that the water would wash away the evil and fear that chilled my body.

When I was done, I got changed and, for the first time in days, left the condo. I didn't bother with a face mask. Didn't care if I got infected or infected others. The demon's affliction was far ghastlier.

I half-expected to find a yellow Volkswagen Beetle in my parking spot, reverse lights on, ready to smash into me. But there was only my car.

So I drove into the night. The lights from traffic lights, cars, shops, restaurants and hawker centres blazed into my eyes.

There was only one place left to go.

I turned at the traffic lights. Other than three stray dogs crossing the bitumen, the street was empty.

I parked my car and got out.

I stood, a half-dead figure, at the Moongate.

Smirking at the inevitability, I entered the walled entrance and darkness, like an old friend, embraced me, its faint earthy decaying smell welcoming me.

The track wended away from all I knew and everything I was. It led me into inky shadows, into the shrills of insects and mysteries unknown. The jungle was breathing, low and deep from the ancient soil, the worms, ants and insects merging into its every breath.

Through the canopy, the full moon glimmered, its corpse-glow on my cheek, drawing me on.

I nodded at it as if we had an understanding.

I'll find that demon.

Maybe Anna would be strolling hand in hand with it.

I will find them.

I'll hike all night if I have to.

But I didn't need to.

For up ahead, like a silhouetted infection on the steep steps, stood two figures draped by sickly midnight trees and that ill-fated moon above. One of them was Anna.

As for me, I was never seen again.

Water Flows Deepest

'We'll be closing in a few weeks.'

Lin glanced up at the supermarket owner who was scratching his grey hair behind the checkout counter.

'So soon?' She placed a finger beneath the scanner which connected with the nano-chip under her skin and paid for her groceries.

'We just don't have enough customers,' he continued. 'Things are quiet around here. How are things on your end? With all that water, I thought everyone would have fled.'

She tried to smile. 'We're hanging on. But most apartment blocks near us are empty now.'

'And you're not leaving?'

Lin glanced at her daughter, Crystal, who was thirteen. She had sprouted in the last year and was as tall as she was. 'We're staying. There's nowhere else for us to go.'

He switched off his visual screen where he had been reading the news. 'What about the flood centres? The government has opened so many of them.'

'They're too crowded. People are crammed into those schools, stadiums and community halls. We'll only go if we're forced to. The conditions there are awful. We'll be living like refugees.'

'I suppose, in the end, that's what we'll all become.' Then he drew closer and Lin smelt cigarettes. He said in a low voice: 'You need to be careful when you go home.'

Lin stared at him.

He frowned. 'You haven't heard?'

'Heard what?'

'The thing in the water.'

'What thing in the water?'

He leaned forward. 'Have you noticed any dogs or cats around lately?'

She shook her head. 'No, I haven't. There used to be plenty around but I thought maybe the owners decided to keep them indoors.'

'That's not the real reason. There used to be many in the streets because they were abandoned by the owners. But then they started to disappear. I thought maybe they just left the area. But then that young boy . . . he was *taken*. He was playing with his father in the flooded football field. You know the one beside the abandoned fishing village?'

Lin felt Crystal take her hand and shot a glance at her.

'Mum, that field is just next to where we live.'

Lin nodded. 'That's right, Crystal, it is.'

'Then you both need to be extra careful. You see, they were playing ball and splashing water at each other. The water was not even knee deep.'

'Oh, we never do that,' Lin said. 'It's dangerous. You know, broken glass, sharp bricks, all kinds of stuff.'

He nodded. 'Anyway, they were playing and then the father saw something in the water, like an oil slick coming towards them. The boy screamed, he fell and was dragged away.'

'What? Dragged away?'

'That's right. As if he was being pulled away by something. The father chased after him. He thought it was a crocodile at first but we don't have them around here. But all he could see was this big dark shadow dragging his son.'

'H-How big?' Crystal asked.

'I don't know, young lady. I doubt it was a shark or a crocodile because they're hardly any left. He saw nothing but darkness, like a black curtain or an oil slick. Then the boy stopped screaming because his head went under and then he was gone.'

Lin shivered. 'When . . . when did this happen?'

'Just last week. His wife came in and told me the story. I put this up for her.' He pointed at a black and white A4-sized poster that Lin had barely glanced at earlier. It read: 'Missing 8-year-old boy' and had a photo of a smiling child. There was a reward and a contact number.

Lin swallowed. She didn't know what she would do if anything happened to Crystal.

'So you two be careful out there.'

'We will. Thanks for warning us.'

Picking up a bag of groceries each, they left the supermarket.

* * *

They strolled down a deserted road.

No vehicles. No people.

Tired grey clouds hung low and Lin wished she was someplace else. But where that could be, she didn't know.

The bitumen was hot and dry but as they got closer to their neighbourhood, it glistened snake-like and there was the usual litter of shells, bits of wood, plastic bottles and polystyrene. Soon came sandbags piled up at crossroads and along fence lines.

Then they were trodding through ankle-deep, then calf-deep water.

'Do people still live here?' Crystal asked, glancing at bungalows sitting in flooded gardens.

'Most have left,' Lin replied. 'The few that remain have abandoned the ground level and live upstairs. They don't want to move into those flood centres.'

Crystal turned to her mother. 'And we're not going either?'

Lin shook her head. 'No, we're not. Don't worry, we'll stay on in the apartment.'

'I wish we could live somewhere else.'

'Well, we're not lucky enough to have relatives who can take us in. Or have enough money to move somewhere else. Rents have shot up everywhere.'

'Do you remember what the man said, mum?' Crystal asked. 'About the thing in the water?'

Crystal frowned and Lin smiled at her reassuringly.

'It's just a story, Crystal. Nothing to be concerned about.'

'But what if it's true?'

'It's not. People like to make up tall tales to amuse themselves.'

'But what about the poster of the missing boy. You saw it.'

'That part is true. The poor boy is missing. His parents must be so worried but that doesn't mean that there's something in the water that grabs people and takes them away. The boy was probably kidnapped.'

Crystal nodded. 'I don't talk to strangers and you're always with me. I don't even go to school now.'

'Home schooling is better, isn't it? Anyway, we're almost home. These groceries are getting heavy.'

They sloshed past several apartment blocks until they reached a drab, grey tower that stood high up against the ashen sky. It was once touted as a luxury seafront condominium but now it was a towering island citadel under constant siege.

The guard house, its walls water-stained, stood empty. The glass screen where visitors once had their faces scanned for identification was shattered and the boom gates were permanently raised as if welcoming any stranger or burglar.

Or kidnapper.

No, Lin didn't want to think of such things. Their lives were tough enough without having to worry about a creature that snatched children.

She took Crystal's hand for the water was deeper here, reaching above their knees and soaking the bottom of their shorts. As they waded up the driveway towards the apartment block, the water lowered down to their calves, then their ankles.

Halfway up the driveway, they were back on dry bitumen. It was littered by sea debris which scattered up past the small roundabout to the lobby and then down to the basement parking. The parking entrance was dark like an open mouth and completely flooded.

Long ago, when there were things worth celebrating, the management used to put up festive greeting decorations in the middle of that roundabout: rotating through Christmas trees, enlarged Hari Raya *ketupats*, Diwali lanterns and a big red lion for Chinese New Year. Strange. She had thought then how odd it was that people still clung to these old celebrations in an age of space tourism and world hunger.

But now bricks and rusty metal rods had been dumped in the middle of the roundabout forming a grotesque sculpture and the only management left was the sea for it now governed their lives.

'Not sure when we can go grocery shopping again,' Lin said as they reached the lobby. 'The tide will be high again soon.'

'Have we got enough food?' Crystal asked.

'I'm sure we do.'

'That's good then'. Crystal said absent-mindedly as she picked up a shell and turned it in her hand. 'This one's pretty. I'm going to keep it.'

As the electricity had been cut off long ago, they climbed the concrete fire stairs as usual. It smelt damp and the mildew on the walls seemed to grow higher by the day. By propping the fire doors open at each level, enough light could spill in for them to climb up the six levels to their apartment unmolested by darkness.

The apartment had once belonged to her father. He had lived there for many years, buying it with his retirement savings when rising tides made prices plummet. The stunning sea view is priceless, he once messaged her. He loved the view across the sea to the majestic mountain, Gunung Jerai, on the Kedah mainland.

When he suffered a stroke, which was a year after her divorce, Lin had to quit her job as a robotics technician and moved in to nurse him. He died four years ago when the major one struck. By then the sea had become an unwelcome visitor which regularly flooded the swimming pool and the basement car park.

'I'm glad we don't live in the penthouse,' Lin wheezed as she placed the grocery bags on the kitchen bench. 'Climbing twenty-five floors wouldn't be much fun.'

'I wished the lifts still worked,' Crystal said, glancing up the many flights of stairs they had to climb. 'Did they turn the power off because we're not supposed to live here?'

Lin nodded. 'The lifts stopped working because of the short circuits caused by the flooding. It was only later that we got the notice to vacate.'

'But why doesn't the government want us to live here?'

'They say it's too dangerous.'

'Is that why everyone's left?'

Lin nodded. 'I suppose so. There's only us and the old Malay couple on the third floor. Did you see their kayak chained up in the lobby?'

'I did. Maybe we need a boat too, mum.'

'Maybe.'

She glanced at their portable gas cooker. 'Let's cook them something. They're old and alone with no one looking after them.'

* * *

'The water's getting higher and higher,' said Fitri.

Salma smiled. 'It's been doing that for years, my love.'

He wore rubber slippers and stood in ankle-deep water in the lobby.

'It's like a lake now,' Fitri added. 'Surrounding us.'

'Remember how we used to catch the ride share from here?' Salma said, pointing to the flooded driveway. She was wearing a white brimmed hat over a red headscarf, to protect her face from the sun.

Fitri sighed. 'That seems such a long time ago. We should have moved when the food delivery drones stopped coming.'

'But that was too late, my love. Nobody wanted our apartment. No matter what discounts we gave. We did try, remember?'

Fitri smiled. 'Yes, of course, I do. I might be seventy-eight but my memory isn't quite gone.'

Salma chuckled. 'I'm not far behind you. But sometimes I can't remember what day it is.'

'Ah, but that's because days aren't important now. It's the tide that tells us whether we can go out or not. Whether we're stuck here or whether we can splash our way to the supermarket.'

'Good thing then that you bought the kayak, my love. We can head out even when the tide is high.'

Fitri nodded. 'Got it at a good price too.'

He propped two sets of paddles against a black metal post and hunched over the kayak chain to unlock it. His back muscles twinged as he bent over. He grimaced but said nothing for Salma would only worry. She worried about so many things these days.

'Is that lock strong enough?' she asked.

'I'm sure it is,' he replied. 'Anyway, I think it's just us and that lady and her daughter left.'

Salma nodded. 'Oh yes, she made us that layer cake.'

Fitri pulled out the chain and looped it over one hand. 'But maybe we do need a stronger lock. We can't take chances.' He had once been an engineer building walls to contain the landslides because of too much rain and knew to take nothing for granted.

The couple took a paddle each and, with some effort, pushed the kayak from the lobby and got into the two cockpits beside the small roundabout with its mess of bricks and iron rods. They paddled towards the guardhouse, floating over the driveway lined with half-submerged lamp posts and palm trees whose fronds were either yellowing or dead and brown.

Fitri knew the deepest part was at the guardhouse where the water was at least five-foot deep. He remembered vehicles endlessly entering and exiting from the main road, the boom gates going up and down. But all was quiet and deserted now. There was just the sound of lapping water. What had happened to it all? As if in reply, a dead fish floated past, one rotting eye staring up at the late afternoon sun.

Don't know, it seemed to say. *Just don't know.*

As they rowed, the water was clear at first but turned murky as they approached a floating island of rubbish. He grimaced as the kayak nosed through plastic, polystyrene, tin cans, bits of wood and dead leaves.

Eventually, they reached a row of abandoned shophouses which once housed a laundrette, a drone courier service, a tele-clinic and an old-fashioned café that served *nasi kandar*. Fitri sighed recalling the meals he ate there with his friends, drinking sweet tea and chatting. His friends had all abandoned the neighbourhood. It was just him and his wife left . . . and this endless water.

When the bottom of the kayak scraped against bitumen, the old couple got out. Fitri chained the kayak to a lamp post and, carrying their paddles, they made the short stroll to the supermarket.

* * *

'Good that the kayak's still here,' Fitri said on their return. 'I was worried it might get stolen.'

'Who would want to steal it, my love?' Salma asked.

'Boats are in big demand now. If the kayak was stolen, we'd have to wade back home with these groceries balanced on our heads.'

Salma giggled, sounding almost like that girl of sixteen when they first met. 'We'd get very wet. But it might be fun.'

'Not my idea of fun, my dear. I'd much rather row back. You know, one day the water is never going to recede and only way in and out in this kayak.'

'I hope we can move by then.'

'But move where? We can't afford to rent anywhere. And I don't want to move to that flood centre. We'll be refugees in our own country.'

'Maybe we'll just have to. Thousands have moved there.'

'Maybe. Only if we have no choice.'

Fitri thought of his two children as he hunched over to unlock the chain and freed the kayak. His armpits were sweaty and his back was worse.

They could have taken us in.

But Nora was lost to a pandemic and Alif died of a heart attack. And their grandchildren couldn't be bothered. Such was life. They just had to get on with it as best they could.

Salma slotted one bag of groceries into each cockpit.

Paddling down the road, they pushed through the large clump of rubbish.

'Almost home,' Fitri said.

The security post was up ahead. It was once manned by two overweight Nepalese guards who had waved at them whenever they arrived home. They had to sell their Mazda when the basement parking began to regularly flood.

Fitri missed that car. He missed life as it used to be. But what was the use of hankering for the past when everything was Allah's will?

They rowed past the security post's water-stained walls, the broken glass screen, the permanently raised boom gates, over the driveway towards the lobby.

'Okay, we can get out here,' Fitri said, stopping the kayak at the small roundabout. 'That's enough rowing for the day.'

'My legs have pins and needles,' Salma said.

'You should have told me.'

'They come and they go, my love. Nothing to worry about.'

Fitri grinned at his wife. 'I always worry about you, my dear.'

He hauled himself out of the front cockpit into the ankle-deep water, feeling the soreness throbbing in his back. It was like an old friend, visiting him from time to time. But it would be some effort to drag the boat to the lobby and chain it up to that metal post.

'What is that?' Salma asked.

He turned to see her seated in the rear cockpit and gesturing behind him.

Fitri frowned. 'I can't see anything . . .'

'Can't you see that dark patch over there? It looks like it's coming towards us. What is it?' Salma leaned forward for a better look.

Fitri squinted at the water. 'Oh, I see it. I'm not sure. Looks like a big oil slick. Or a black curtain in the water.'

'I don't like it, my love. Can you hear it? It sounds like . . . like someone breathing.'

'Yes, yes, I hear something. But I'm sure it's nothing to worry about, my dear. Let me have a look.'

'D-don't go near it, please.'

'Oh, don't worry.' Fitri took several steps towards the floating darkness and squinted at this strange black curtain.

His eyesight was not good but he guessed that it was probably an oil slick. As it drew closer and his eyes could focus better, he knew that it wasn't one because it floated not on water but rather *below* it.

'Much too big to be a crocodile or shark,' he muttered beneath his breath. 'The shape's all wrong.'

'What is it, my love?' Salma called from behind him.

'Not sure yet,' he replied. 'Maybe a large shoal of fish.'

But he didn't think that was right either.

It moved in a strange way, glimmering and wavering like a black fog filled with dangerous creatures beneath the sunlight. It reminded him of a nightmare he once had. He was in a bed and a huge black cloak fell from the ceiling, smothering him in cold darkness. He gasped out loud only to find Salma still asleep. But this was no nightmare, it was right here.

As he stared, the breathing sound grew louder. The water began to ripple around him.

His throat went dry. His chest quivered.

There was a smell. Of dust and smoke and dead things.

This curtain-like fog swept towards him, withdrawing and darting forward in an almost slow taunting way, getting bigger as it did so.

He gasped as sudden coldness grasped his slippered feet.

Inky darkness surrounded his legs, swirling around his ankles.

Blood drained from his face.

'Fitri!' he heard Salma yelling, but it echoed from far away. 'Come back here!'

'Salma . . .' he whispered.

Then something grabbed both his ankles and tugged hard. He cried out as his head hit the water.

Bubbles rose from his mouth as he gasped for breath. He tasted salt, a hint of diesel and charcoal.

Salma was screaming but her voice was muffled as if a cloth clogged her mouth. He was dragged through water, arms uselessly flailing. Darkness embraced him, spilling into his eyes, ears and nostrils.

* * *

There was a banging on the front door.

Lin opened it to see the old woman's stricken face. Her white-brimmed hat crammed over her red headscarf flopped over her forehead and loose skin trembled about her cheeks.

'M-My husband!' Salma cried, breathing hard. 'You have to help. H-He's gone. Taken by something. S-Something in the water.'

'What do you mean?'

'We were coming back from the supermarket. Fitri just got out of the kayak when something pulled him under water and dragged him away!'

'Oh no!' Lin stared, mouth open. 'Stay here, Crystal. Don't go anywhere until I come back.'

'But I want to help, mum,' she pleaded.

'No, you can't do that. It might be dangerous. Please just wait here.'

Salma grabbed Lin's arm. 'I paddled out to look for him but I couldn't find him. I was so scared.'

'We'll look again,' Lin said.

They hurried down the fire escape into the flooded lobby.

'Over there,' Salma said, splashing past the kayak and pointing to a patch of water just beyond the small roundabout. 'This black shadow came towards us. Fitri went to have a closer look and the thing . . . it just took him!'

Tears spilled down Salma's cheeks and she sobbed. 'What can I do? How can I find him? Please tell me.'

Lin wasn't sure what happened to Fitri. Perhaps he had just fallen into the water and drowned. She couldn't believe some shadow in the water had dragged him in. It had to be a stroke or heart attack.

Then she remembered what the supermarket owner had told her. She thought he was making up some story. But what if he wasn't?

'I'll take the kayak and look for him,' Lin said. 'You wait here.'

'No, no,' Salma said. 'I-I'll come with you. Maybe I missed something the first time I went out to look.'

They scrambled into the kayak, Lin at front and Salma at the back.

As Lin tried to get used to paddling, she gazed into the hazy water and scanned the water's rippling surface in all directions. She glanced behind the trunks of the palm trees and foliage sticking out of the water lining both sides of the driveway, but there was only the usual floating debris.

'Where could he be?' Salma asked. 'Where . . . where is my husband?'

'I don't know. Let's have a look on the main road.'

They paddled past the abandoned guardhouse. A crow perched on top of the boom gate, staring down at them. Then it cawed and flew so close past Lin that she felt the beat of its wings on her face.

'Stupid bird,' she gasped. 'Why did it do that?'

'They're getting daring,' Salma said. 'With no humans around.'

Lin had recently seen a monitor lizard swimming about the lobby. Instead of fleeing when it saw her, it simply turned its glistening head and stared as if chastising her for staying when everyone had left.

They found nothing but floating litter on the main road. Turning back to the apartment, they paddled over the once-manicured gardens, now drowned. Several trees had bare branches whilst others desperately held onto their dropping, sickly foliage.

Over the remains of the swimming pool, the kayak bounced upon the small waves rolling in from the sea. They searched along the metal fence lined with dead palm trees which once separated the apartment grounds from the esplanade gardens where people had strolled their dogs and children chased each other. All now lay submerged and the fence poked out a miserable two feet from the water, a lonely barrier between them and the sea.

'He's not anywhere!' Salma cried, striking the back of the plastic kayak repeatedly with one hand.

The thudding sounded like heavy soil falling on a coffin. But Muslims, Lin knew, didn't use a coffin, just a white shroud tucked into the earth. The old man had neither, just a watery grave.

'My husband is dead,' the old woman moaned, as she continued to strike the hollow plastic. 'I saw him go in. He can't be alive. Not now. We've looked everywhere.'

Lin's heart ached for Salma. She glanced up at a sky carpeted by shadows and frowned. 'Let's go back. We can search again tomorrow.'

The old woman stopped her thudding and nodded. 'Yes, yes . . . it's starting to get dark.'

They turned the kayak around.

When they reached the lobby, Lin helped the old woman out of the cockpit.

Salma's face was tired and distraught. She seemed so weak, so helpless standing there, as water lapped about her thin ankles.

'If only my son and daughter . . .' she said, her voice quivering. 'If only they were still alive, we wouldn't be stuck here. We would've had somewhere to go.'

Lin didn't know what to say. What words could she use to comfort her? Telling her all would be okay would have been an outright lie.

Nothing was going to be okay. For any of them.

'Mum?'

She turned around to see Crystal.

'What are you doing here? I told you to wait at home.'

'But I wanted to see,' Crystal said. 'I thought I could help.'

Lin sighed. 'We looked everywhere. There was no sign of him.'

'Come with us,' she said to Salma, her voice softening. 'I'll make you some tea and something to eat.'

Salma squeezed her eyes shut, placed her head on Lin's shoulder and sobbed.

* * *

'How was she?' Crystal asked.

'Very sad,' Lin sighed, looking up from her book. 'She wept most of the time when we were talking. She liked the pancake you made for her though.'

Lin was sitting at the dining table by the balcony sliding door and Crystal was hovering in the kitchen.

'I used up all the powdered milk,' Crystal said, turning to her mother. 'What really happened to her husband, mum?'

Lin sighed. 'I don't really know. Maybe he had a stroke or a heart attack, fell in the water and drowned.'

'But what about his body? You both couldn't find it.'

'I'm not sure. Maybe he was taken away by the tide. Or maybe a crocodile took his body.'

'But you said there are almost no crocodiles left. Maybe it was that dark patch of . . .'

'I don't want to hear that nonsense. Anything can happen with sea levels rising. Islands and whole nations have disappeared. There're new diseases, drought and famine. Food is getting so expensive. I'm sorry, this isn't the kind of world I wished for you.'

'It's okay, mum,' Crystal said, turning to the bedroom. 'We'll all be fine in the end.'

Lin was surprised by her daughter's optimism. But it was misplaced. Things would only get worse. Much worse.

She gazed out at the waves lapping against the building below, listening to its rhythmic sound, the angled tower block's shadow like a hungry giant over the water.

The water stretched out in muddy coloured patches threaded through by long lines of sea foam. It was this same sea that had slowly swallowed everything up. Swallowed up their lives.

On those stunning shots on social media, it seemed a beautiful friend. She didn't like to think of it as an enemy, but that was what it had sadly become.

In the distance, beneath a swarm of delivery drones a lone container ship like a ghost cruised towards the new floating port north of Prai on the mainland, built to withstand rising sea levels. There were no more fishing boats for the seas around here had been emptied of them.

She turned back to her book. It was a tattered, yellowing copy of Tolstoy's *War and Peace*, taken from her father's bookshelf. It was the sort of book you read when you had time on your hands which was all she seemed to have now.

She lit a kerosene lamp as darkness fell and continued reading in its yellow glow, then stopped at a sentence.

'Let's borrow the kayak tomorrow,' she called out.

Crystal sauntered out of the bedroom. 'What did you say, mum?'

'I said we'll borrow her kayak tomorrow. For food shopping. We should do some for her too. She's frail and she'll need help now that her husband's gone.'

'Yes, mum. We should do that.'

'We'll go tomorrow then.'

She turned back to the novel and re-read the words:

. . . *water flows deepest where the land lies lowest.*

* * *

The next morning, Lin went to see Salma but found a furry black rat crouched at her front door instead. She shooed the thing away but not before the rat gave her a furtive, knowing glance before darting away. The old woman wasn't home and so she went down the fire escape to look for her.

Lin splashed through the lobby's ankle-deep water and, beneath the grey sky, rain covered the water in dark ripples. Then she noticed that the kayak was missing.

She turned her head to a dull thudding coffin-like sound.

Something red bobbed against the guardhouse, hitting the wall. It was the kayak, turned upside down.

Floating beside it like a rotting flower was Salma's white wide-brimmed hat.

'No!'

Lin's first instinct was to splash past the small roundabout and plunge into the water. But where was the old woman? There was no sign of her.

'Where are you?' Lin gasped. 'Did you try to go grocery shopping by yourself? Or were you looking for your husband's body?'

Any why did the kayak flip over?

Was she attacked by a crocodile? That was the most likely reason for there were no big waves here. She was certain that Salma was dead, perhaps floating head down in the water somewhere.

Breath spilled from her throat as loss overcame her. It was that same feeling she had when she was speeding down the expressway when she got news of her father's stroke. She had seen three clumps of mangled fur, dead monkeys hit by cars. Further along were two shrieking monkeys on the roadside, cars shooting by them, and all around stood oil palm plantations. Cold, lifeless, indifferent. She felt like crying then and she felt like it now.

As she blinked and turned away, her eyes caught onto something floating against the apartment block, darkly embracing it beneath the grey tear-filled sky. It was a big black patch floating on the building's side. She thought it was an oil slick at first but as she stared she realized that it lay beneath the murky rippling water and yet, as she watched, it seemed to grow larger before her eyes as if it was waiting to be observed.

The shadow was spreading like an infestation and she thought she heard a low breathing sound.

Her face went cold.

Whatever this was, was now moving.

It slowly, deliberately slid through the water like a black curtain being pulled or a blob being sucked away.

Then it vanished into a dark cave-like hole.

It was the entrance of the flooded basement parking.

'So that's where you've been hiding,' Lin whispered. 'Whatever you are, you're real!'

* * *

From the balcony, Lin gazed down at the metal fencing and dead palms that once separated the apartments from the esplanade. The fence line was her tide-level marker. But she ventured down at least twice a day to see for herself but, as always, the tide was too high, the water lapping against the lobby tiles, making a low sucking sound.

Too dangerous, she thought.

The body of water was an unwelcome visitor that didn't know how to leave. It covered the entire driveway and darkly gleamed at the entrance of the basement car park as if watching her.

Her heart skipped a beat. *Far, far too dangerous.*

Then almost a week after Salma went missing, when they were surviving on white rice and sachets of tomato sauce, she rushed back into the apartment.

'We're going today,' she blurted.

Crystal frowned. 'Are you sure, mum?'

'The tide's low enough. Let's go.'

'Was it like the last time we went to the supermarket, mum?'

'Yes, it's just like that. This is what we've been waiting for.'

They picked up their backpacks, which they had been packed days ago. Lin glanced out of the balcony door at the expanse of sea, the hazy sky, at Gunung Jerai, now blanketed in clouds. She took a deep breath and stepped out of the apartment.

At the lobby, the water had slipped back to half way down the driveway.

Lin stared at the basement parking entrance. The ramp leading to it was dry. She was sure that the thing, whatever it was, would be stuck there with the abandoned cars.

It's no different from a fish, she thought. *It always needs water.*

She turned to Crystal. She hadn't mentioned the thing that hid there and she wasn't going to say anything. There was no need to frighten her.

She squeezed Crystal's shoulder and they set off down the driveway. They skirted the small roundabout, went past the scattered debris, sickly-looking palm trees and dead shrubs. Then they were in calf-deep water and, at the guard house, it reached above their knees. There was no sign of the kayak.

'Why do you keep looking behind you?' Crystal asked.

Lin shrugged. 'No real reason.'

'We're leaving for good, aren't we, mum?'

Lin adjusted the straps on her backpack. 'Yes . . . yes, we are. We've no choice now.'

Crystal nodded, sadness on her face.

As they went past the guard house, Lin stole a final look up the driveway.

Still no sign of it.

She felt she could breathe again.

The water was calf-deep on the main road. With each step she took, that brooding heavy feeling of the last few days began to lift. Perhaps the conditions at the flood centre wouldn't be so bad. There was always hope.

As mother and daughter left their home behind, the water began to rise at the basement carpark entrance. It crept up the ramp like a stealthy animal onto the driveway, gurgling as it encircled the small roundabout before spilling down the bitumen towards the guardhouse. Together with the rising water came a breathing darkness that spread itself out. A vast black cloak, it neither resembled a huge shoal of fish or a team of lurking crocodiles for it kept changing like a black mist with grotesque creatures slipping in and out of it.

It followed mother and daughter at a distance.

If they had glanced back they would have seen a wall of water rising high behind them, moving in a slow surging motion, flooding homes and shophouses, pushing over shrubs and trees, overwhelming mosques, temples, churches, washing away cars, dustbins, lamp posts, animals and even people.

It stopped when mother and daughter entered the supermarket. It waited, unmoving, like crashing water in a tattered photograph or a great wave on a Japanese print.

'We're closing next week,' said the supermarket owner. His wrinkles seemed to have etched deeper beneath his grey hair and his eyes were weary.

'That's just as well then,' Lin said. 'We're going to the flood centre. Just picking up a few things we might need there.'

'It's high time you left. It's very wet down there. Someday soon we'll get flooded too.'

He didn't mention the thing in the water. Nor did she.

'Best of luck to you both,' he added.

'You too,' Lin replied, picking up her bag of provisions.

'Bye,' Crystal said. 'Thank you.'

He nodded at them as they left the supermarket and returned to the news. If he had turned to glance out of the window, he would have seen a dark wall of water moving slowly and irrevocably towards him.

Mother and daughter strolled up the slope and entered a road busy with vehicles.

Lin stared. It was a strange sight to see traffic again and it felt as if the world was carrying on unchanged.

They didn't have to wait long for the bus.

It was half full with passengers. Several had large bags and were, like them, destined for the nearest flood centre.

Crystal opened her palm to reveal a seashell she had been holding. It glittered in the sunlight.

Lin stared out of the window, lost in one thought.

'. . . *water flows deepest where the land lies lowest.*'

No one looked back to see its shadow rising in the distance, slowly following them.